PUCKER

For Kaitlin,

P U C K E R

Best Wishes!

MELANIE GIDEON

razor
bill

Pucker

RAZORBILL

Published by the Penguin Group
Penguin Young Readers Group
345 Hudson Street, New York, New York 10014, U.S.A.
Penguin Group (USA) Inc., 375 Hudson Street, New York,
New York 10014, U.S.A.
Penguin Group (Canada), 90 Eglinton Avenue, Suite 700, Toronto,
Ontario, Canada M4P 2Y3 (a division of Pearson Penguin Canada Inc.)
Penguin Books Ltd, 80 Strand, London WC2R 0RL, England
Penguin Ireland, 25 St Stephen's Green, Dublin 2,
Ireland (a division of Penguin Books Ltd)
Penguin Group (Australia), 250 Camberwell Road, Camberwell,
Victoria 3124, Australia (a division of Pearson Australia Group Pty Ltd)
Penguin Books India Pvt Ltd, 11 Community Centre, Panchsheel Park,
New Delhi - 110 017, India
Penguin Group (NZ), Cnr Airborne and Rosedale Roads, Albany,
Auckland 1310, New Zealand (a division of Pearson New Zealand Ltd)
Penguin Books (South Africa) (Pty) Ltd, 24 Sturdee Avenue,
Rosebank, Johannesburg 2196, South Africa

Penguin Books Ltd, Registered Offices: 80 Strand, London WC2R 0RL, England

10 9 8 7 6 5 4 3 2 1

Library of Congress Cataloging-in-Publication Data is available

Printed in the United States of America

FOR BENJAMIN H. REWIS

PUCKER

· PART ·
ONE

ONE

LET ME SAY THIS RIGHT up front: this is not a story about kissing, or wrinkles, or things that are sour. It's a story about redemption. I suppose all stories are, and if they're not, well, then they should be. For what else do we have in the end—but hope?

I walk into my mother's room and try not to breathe. The air smells stale and musty, like cardboard boxes. She hates it when I assume she needs assistance, so I stand there like some sort of teenage butler with a tray in my hands. Lately she's been complaining that all her joints ache like somebody reassembled her bones while she slept. I inch forward and she holds up her palm, warding me away. Chronic pain, like undressing or going to the bathroom, is a private matter. Finally she manages to prop herself up. She pats the blanket, signaling that she's ready for her breakfast, and I slide the tray across her lap.

I know what she's thinking: eggs *again*. It's hard to come up with new ideas when I've been preparing my mother breakfast, lunch, and dinner every day since I turned eleven.

"There was another crank call last night," she says. She carefully separates the white of the egg from the yolk. "They asked for Pucker."

I shrug. The name isn't news to me.

"Why do you let them call you that?"

She's not inquiring; she's accusing me, as if I have some say in what my classmates have nicknamed me.

"Because it's true," I say.

I'm a burn victim. My scars are primarily on my face. My skin is either unnaturally smooth or, yes, puckered. It's the best the plastic surgeons can do, this face that I have finally arrived at.

"Do you want to know the etymology of *Pucker*?" I ask. This is a rhetorical question; I'm sure she doesn't, but I feel a need to dig at her.

Well, first let's get the obvious out of the way—yes, I know what it rhymes with. It comes from the Old English *pouke*: variations *poake*, *puckle*, and *pug*. Alternately described as a fairy, a goblin, a brownie, or an elf. I don't attach myself to any of these. Too effeminate, except for the goblin. What I take from the definition is that I'm a shape-shifter. And it's true: I shift shapes all the time. Look, here's me being a parent. And here's me hiding underneath my Shoei helmet, pretending to be a strapping young man, and here's me in the mirror, a seventeen-year-old with the face of a wizened geriatric.

Suddenly I realize my mother's gotten dressed. She's wearing a red sweater instead of her usual quilted housecoat. She's also made a crude attempt at fixing herself up, but a sizable chunk of hair juts out from her head like a corkscrew. Her pathetic effort worries me. I flip the light switch so I can see her better.

"No," she barks, shielding her eyes. I quickly turn it off, but not before I've gotten a look at her face. She's wearing makeup.

"Are you going somewhere?" My mother hasn't left the house in over seven years.

"No, but I'm hoping you are," she says.

She picks at her breakfast in silence and I don't force the conversation. This isn't unusual. In some homes silence can be a killing thing, a murderous and bloody weapon. In our house silence is a lodger, a permanent guest: well behaved, never eating more than his share, but always lurking nearby.

"I'll be dead in less than a month," she says a few minutes later. "If I'm to live, you've got to go back to Isaura and find my skin."

TWO

GO BACK TO ISAURA—SHE might as well have told me to walk to the North Pole and find Santa Claus.

Isaura. It sounds familiar, doesn't it? A tiny country nestled between Armenia and Turkey? An island in the Caspian Sea? I'm afraid it's a bit more complicated than that. Isaura is not a country: it's another world. Well, more like a pocket of a world.

Think of Earth as an old dog. Despite its age, the dog is vibrant and healthy. Yet on its flanks and belly there are all sorts of lumps and growths that come from being billions of years old. The lumps are benign and cause the dog no pain. In fact, the dog is unaware of their presence, much in the same way it would be unaware if a tick were embedded in the soft flesh behind its ear. But these lumps and growths are much more than fatty deposits. They are, in fact, parallel realities. Isaura, where my mother and I come from, is one of these growths.

A few hundred years ago you might not have been able to tell the two realities apart. Both were on the same trajectory, advancing at similar rates. Back then there were portals between Isaura and Earth—actually, between Isaura and various points on the North American continent—but the traveling was strictly one-way. Isaurians came and went as they pleased. North Americans had no clue that Earth had a doppelganger; a sister world clinging to theirs like a parasite.

Isaurian scholars learned many things from their

travels to Earth, the main lesson being that there was little difference between the inhabitants of the two worlds except for one thing: some Isaurians could see into the future.

Before the Great War, this ability to see into the future was nothing special; in fact, it was seen as a disability. Only a small percentage of Isaurians were Seers, and most of them tried never to use their powers because it made them outsiders, privy to things they had no right to know. Unfortunately for them, there was no hiding their identities, because when they were teenagers, all Seers grew second skins, golden-tinged, translucent ones.

It was only a matter of time before somebody realized that there was a profit to be made off the Seers. Soon the wealthiest of Isaurians put the Seers to work and with their help increased the size of their fortunes. Within fifty years' time a wide chasm had grown between those who could afford the services of the Seers and those who could not, and one night a mob of angry farmers massacred a group of Seers while they were sleeping in their beds. It was the beginning of the Great War.

Casting about for someone to blame for this horrific act, Isaurians pointed the finger at Earth, particularly America. It was easy to believe our host had poisoned us. American society focused solely on the future and measured success by the attainment of material possessions. It was America's ambition and hunger that swept through the portals and infected us all.

The portals were immediately shut. But even then, the barbarity went on, and, really, we had nobody to blame but ourselves after that. Soon, instead of killing the Seers, a far more sadistic form of torture was concocted. The Seers were flayed of their second skins and the skins were cut up and sold. It was said that whoever got a piece of a stolen Seer skin would be able to see the future. The wretched Seers who were stripped of their skins lost their sight forever—and their lives, too, more often than not.

In response, the Ministry was formed, an agency that dedicated itself to protecting the surviving Seers and distributing knowledge of the future equally to everyone, regardless of ability to pay. Now everything would be predicted and nothing would be left to chance. From weather to crops, from marriages to friendships, illnesses, even talents—it would all be forecast. Crops would never fail, children wouldn't get caught in the rain, nobody would ever enter into a relationship that wouldn't stand the test of time, and it was in this way that peace once again came to Isaura.

It was this way for 152 years. Until the day the horror started all over again . . .

THREE

BARKER'S JUVENILE PRIMER NO. 3
Containing pertinent moral and historical lessons
for the edification and improvement
of all Isaurian children

I STARED AT THE BOOK with a mixture of hate and fascination. This was my anchor and my touchstone, this brown leather–bound book that was issued to every Isaurian child at birth. Every hour of every day, if you walked down any street or eavesdropped on any conversation, you would hear mothers and fathers saying to their children, "Look it up in Barker's."

Barker's was the third parent in every Isaurian household. Parents adored it, for it saved them endless hours of explanation. Children hated it, for they disliked nothing more than being told to go look something up when what they expressly wanted was a quick answer. But at eight years old I was well acquainted with Mr. Barker and his juvenile primer.

I snapped open the spine of the book and riffled through it quickly. I already knew some of the pages by heart. Page two was the first thing Isaurian children had to memorize. I could have recited it underwater, standing on one foot, even while doing arithmetic.

1. *He comes along without being told.*
2. *He is strong of limb. He has a hearty appetite, but he does not take the last chicken leg left on the platter.*
3. *He is never without his Barker's.*
4. *He does not commune with the Changed.*
5. *His hands are washed, his teeth brushed, his hair combed, and his clothing clean before he enters the Ministry each morning.*
6. *He is quiet at all times in the Ministry, especially while his future is being read.*
7. *He strives at all times to be impartial.*
8. *He is thrifty in all matters.*
9. *He is prepared.*

I was unprepared when my mother entered the kitchen. It was early Saturday morning and the sun wasn't even up; the world was mine and mine alone. I wouldn't have known she was there if it hadn't been for her lemony smell floating into the room. My mother glanced over my shoulder and gave a disapproving shake of her head when she saw I was reading Barker's.

"Out—it's a beautiful day," she said.

"It's still dark," I said.

She had a distracted and faraway look on her face, as if she couldn't be bothered with things like sunrise.

I tapped the page with my finger to show her what I was studying.

"Obedient children are boring children," she remarked.

She was holding a bowl full of plums. This afternoon Cook would make a cobbler from those plums, for every Saturday night we had company—a group of my parents' fellow Seers came to our house. When the Seers came, I was sent to my room. I tried to eavesdrop, but the walls were too thick. I loved Saturday nights because I was allowed to stay up late. As long as I didn't disrupt their dinner, I could do whatever I wanted.

"You have one hour. You need to wash," my mother began.

"His hands are washed, his teeth brushed, his hair combed, and his clothing clean before he enters the Ministry each morning," I recited.

It seemed to displease my mother that I had committed "The Obedient Child" to memory. She frowned and left the room.

I thought my mother, Serena, was the most beautiful Seer in all of Isaura and my father, William, the handsomest. Their Seerskins made them glisten and sparkle, as if there were hundreds of tiny stars sewn into their flesh. I couldn't keep from touching them, trying to figure out how their skins were attached; was there a seam somewhere? Most of the time they pushed me away. I was too old for this kind of behavior, and in Isaura showing affection in public or in private was frowned on.

I also think my parents didn't want me to feel bad. They didn't want me to focus on the fact that I was an ordinary little boy. The children of Seers had better-than-average chances of becoming Seers themselves, but I had displayed none of the early signs of prophesy. I made grand predictions and pronouncements all the time, but more often than not I was wrong. It was becoming clear to everybody that I had inherited none of my parents' gifts. Still, that did not diminish my fascination with all things related to Seers. If anything, it increased it.

I turned to page 52 in my Barker's. With my finger I traced the caption under the woodcut: *Seer flayed of his skin.*

I had spent hours examining this illustration. It was a battleground scene that had taken place during the Great War. Dozens of Seers, newly flayed of their skins, lay sprawled on the ground, gasping for breath, their limbs contorted into grotesque positions. In the background men in ragged clothes were climbing up into the hills. From their pitchforks dangled the Seers' limp skins.

My mother gasped. Once again I had no idea she had come back into the kitchen. She snatched the book away from me. She was weeping.

I had never, not once in my life, seen her cry. Nor had I ever cried myself, at least not since I was an infant. The Obedient Child never emoted. If he did, his parents would have to turn him in to the Ministry, for this would be the end of our civilization. That's what every schoolchild thought. Emotion, specifically envy, was what had started the Great War. But there was no need for envy any longer because everybody in Isaura got the same thing. Jealousy had no place in a society where everybody was safeguarded from misfortune.

My mother grabbed me by the shoulders and shook me brutally—so hard I began to cry.

"Wake up!" she shouted.

I had no idea what she was talking about. I clawed at her, trying to get her off me.

My father ran into the room. "Serena!"

My mother stared at me like she had no idea who I was and abruptly let go. I ran to my father.

"That's good, Thomas," my father said slowly. He looked at my mother, stunned at my show of emotion and hers. "Let it out," he told me in the same awkward tone of voice he might have used if I were throwing up.

I was bewildered. I had no idea what was going on, but whatever was happening, it was happening to all three of us. It was as if that flayed Seer from my book had jumped out of the pages and into our kitchen and contaminated us all. After the Great War they'd had to build asylums to house the Seers whose skins had been stolen. The Seers couldn't see the future anymore and it had driven them mad. It was said their madness was contagious.

My mother wiped her tearstained cheeks with her fingers and extended her hand to my father, showing him the wetness. "Look, Will," she said, her voice trembling.

He shook his head at her angrily, then knelt in front of me. I buried my face in his chest. Slowly his hands crept around me and he kissed my forehead. This was another first. I had never in my memory been kissed by either of my parents.

My mother turned her attention back to the woodcut of the slain Seers and her face darkened. "I should tear that page out."

"No," I said. "It's my book!" It was the only thing I owned.

·   ·   ·

An hour later my mother and I set out for the Ministry. When we got there, I went into the Children's Room and my mother continued down the corridor. Because my parents were Seers, they didn't have to wait in line with the rest of the population to get their futures read. They were allowed to forecast for each other, and they did this each morning at the breakfast table. They couldn't forecast for me, however, because Seers were unable to see the future of their blood kin.

Morning was a busy time, and ten Seers were working the Children's Room. Each of them had a queue that was a dozen children deep. I sighed and got in line. What I really wanted to do was roam the halls of the Ministry to try and catch a glimpse of the Maker.

The Maker was a relatively new breed of Seer. The first one had come into existence just after the Great War, and there was never more than one at a time. The most astounding thing about the Maker was not that she saw into the past instead of the future, but that she could *change* a person's past. It was because of the Maker that we eventually opened up the portals to Earth again.

Everything had changed, though. No longer were we satisfied with information-gathering expeditions. Now we trolled the streets of America with just one intent: to enlist a workforce for Isaura. Maybe we reasoned that it was payback for the ills that had been inflicted on our society.

It's not as bad as it sounds. We did have codes of conduct. Enlistment was voluntary. We never forced anyone to come. We also only recruited those who were ill, whose bodies were disfigured in some way. In exchange for the Maker healing them, altering the event that had led to their deformity, the Changed (as we came to call them) washed our clothes, cleaned our outhouses, and swept our streets.

I was desperate to see the Maker work her magic—all of us children were. Instead I was stuck listening to the Seers in the Children's Room, who were doing the most mundane of jobs.

"There's a pothole on Cherry Lane; make sure you avoid it. If you don't, you'll sprain your ankle."

"Don't eat the stewed pears; they'll give you a stomachache."

"You're going to fail your history test. I suggest you study a little harder."

These Seers were the workhorses of the Ministry, many of them very young and still apprenticing. When it came to forecasting the daily events that would befall the citizens of Isaura, Seers were limited in their powers. First of all, they couldn't just see somebody's future at whim. They had to be actually touching that person. Also, they could only see out about twenty-four hours at a time. That was why everybody had to come each morning to the Ministry to be read.

With bigger life issues, like vocations, marriage, and births, Seers could see far out into the future, but not with the same level of detail with which they forecast the day's events. Seers could also see years ahead with storms, natural catastrophes, and diseases.

My parents both worked in Weather. They knew that 324 days from now there would be a blizzard that would blanket the countryside with ten feet of snow. Because of their predictions preparations were already under way: food was being stockpiled, and wood had been chopped and stacked in barns.

Finally I got to the front of the line and stuck my hand out eagerly. Given my parents' odd behavior this morning, I was anxious to hear what the rest of the day would hold. The Seer placed his palm on mine and I readied myself for the odd sensation of being read. It felt like hands creeping around inside you, as if your chest were a bureau and the Seer were pushing aside your liver and your spleen, looking for a lost pair of socks. I had been taught that at the exact moment when my breath caught in my throat, I must surrender myself to the Seer's probe. The sensation was like falling.

Only this time I didn't fall. I heard my mother's voice in my head. She yelled my name—"Thomas!"—and I felt the Seer's energy dissipate inside me and scurry away.

The Seer dropped my hand. "Strange," he said.

"What?"

"Nothing." He picked up his notebook and scribbled something next to my name.

"I didn't do anything wrong," I said, worried that he somehow knew what had happened that morning. That I had cried. That my mother had cried. That my father had kissed me.

"Nobody said you did," he said, flicking his hand impatiently at me. "It's my job to report when I can't read somebody. Now move aside, please."

My mother was waiting for me in the hallway. "I want to show you something," she said.

She grabbed my hand, then let it go. She had forgotten herself. Parents did not hold children's hands in Isaura. We wound our way up two staircases and down a hall. Finally we stood in front of an unmarked door. From her pocket she produced a key, and quickly we let ourselves in. We were in a tiny library. My mother breathed deeply. The room smelled of leather.

"Do you know where these books are from, Thomas?" she asked.

I shook my head.

"Can you take a guess?"

I pulled a book from the shelf and read the title—*Anna Karenina*.

"They're from Earth," she told me.

Quickly I slid the book back onto the shelf as if it were diseased. I had been taught that anything from Earth was contaminated, poison. Isaurian children were not even allowed to speak to the Changed.

"Do you want to know how many of these books I've read?" my mother asked.

"No, thank you," I said. This day was getting stranger and stranger. I just wanted to go home.

She stuck her face in mine. "Don't believe what they tell you about Earth, Thomas. It's not a horrible place. It's not filled with savages. Literature like this could only come from a world where there's love."

"What's happened to you?" I asked.

She smoothed the hair back from my forehead. "I don't want to frighten you, baby."

"Then don't call me baby," I said.

•　•　•

My mother took me home. A few hours later there was a knock on our door. Two of the Changed stood on our doorstep, a young girl and a man. They looked similar, with the same silvery blond hair. They wore baskets strapped around their necks; their wares were displayed to their best advantage. We already knew that they were bringing ripe tomatoes, garlic, and a leg of lamb: the Meals Department had determined that more than a week ago.

"The strawberries are ripe today. I've got a fine leg of lamb," said the girl. "Butterflied, just as you wanted it."

She curtsied, but there was no eye contact. She knew the rules. She was not to address me. Isaurian children were considered impressionable and vulnerable. They should have as few dealings with the Changed as possible.

The Changed were good at following the rules, for they lived under threat of being changed back to their disfigured forms and sent back to Earth.

"My son wants chicken," my mother said. "It's his birthday."

That was a lie.

The man looked at us blankly. "But we were told you wanted lamb."

He wasn't trying to be insolent. He was following orders. According to his delivery list, which had been compiled by the Ministry seven days ago, the Gale family would be having a lamb dinner tonight.

"Chicken," my mother challenged him.

"This has never happened before," he said, addressing me.

"Mom," I said, but she stared at me emptily.

The man turned to the girl. "Do we have chickens back in the Compound?"

"Yes," she said.

"I don't want chicken. Lamb is fine," I said.

The girl was pretty, just a few years older than me. Her skin was the color of toffee. What had she looked like before? Were her hands flippers? Was her body curled up into the shape of a comma?

"Lamb is not fine," said my mother, gathering up her sweater.

Twenty minutes later we stood on a hill looking down at the bustling Compound.

"What's your name?" my mother asked the man.

"Ethan 434," he said. 434—his last name: the number of days he'd been in Isaura. Tomorrow his name would change and he'd be Ethan 435.

"Thank you, Ethan 434," she said.

Ethan led us down the hill and we trailed after him like sheep. We went past the bakery and the laundry. I smelled seared cotton and bleach, tallow, fried onions, and yeast.

Our presence in the Compound was unnerving, and the Changed hurried to fulfill my mother's request. They did a sloppy job. The heads of two chickens were lopped off; they were wrapped in a rag and tied with twine. Within minutes the rag and my mother's shirt were maroon with blood. Ethan 434 made no offer to help. I untied the package and ripped off the rag. We used the twine to harness the chickens' feet together and my mother carried them upside down. By the time we got home, they would be drained of their blood.

"Lead me out, quickly now," my mother said.

Ethan 434 led us into the central courtyard, where we stumbled on a cartload of immigrants who had just arrived from America. Some were propped up on pillows, their arms and legs twisted in unthinkable ways. There was a small bald girl who was so emaciated you could see every bone, and a young woman with no legs. But this wasn't why I stared, why I couldn't turn away. It was their gaze. It beat out of them like wings. Was this what my mother had been talking about? Was this what living in a world with love did to you? They looked so *alive*. My mother and I walked closer to the cart.

One of the immigrants stuck her fingers out of the cart

and wiggled them. "Is somebody there?" she called out.

"I'm here," my mother said. Their fingers touched.

"I'm scared," the girl whispered.

I could tell from her voice that she couldn't be more than a teenager.

My mother read her future quickly. "Don't be."

Forecasting her future was something my mother wouldn't be able to do after the girl was Changed. For some reason, once the Maker had molecularly changed an immigrant's past, his or her future became unreadable.

"Will I see you again?" the girl asked.

"I don't think so," my mother told her.

Then my mother brought the girl's fingers to her lips and kissed them. A gasp rippled through the crowd. The Changed had never seen an Isaurian show affection.

I looked across the clearing and saw a man leaning against a pillar, smoking a cigar. He nodded at me. I pointed him out to my mother.

"He's what they call a Host," she explained. "His job is to guide the new recruits through orientation."

"But he doesn't look Changed," I said. I was used to the expressionless, subservient Changed who delivered our food and raised our cattle.

"He's Changed. But there's something different about Hosts. Something the Maker does to them, I think," my mother said. "They're the Ministry's watchdogs," she added with a frown.

"Can I help you?" the Host called out, exhaling a plume of smoke. My heart began to pound its distress. Even though it would draw even more attention to us, I took my mother's hand and squeezed it.

"No, thank you," said my mother calmly. "We got the wrong order. We thought it'd be faster to come and exchange it ourselves."

The Host raised his eyebrows and took a step toward us. "There is no such thing as a wrong order," he said. The crowd dispersed. He squinted, as if he were trying to memorize our faces.

When we got back home, it was late afternoon and Cook was sitting at the kitchen table chopping up the plums into tiny pieces. I could tell by the way she slammed the knife down into the cutting board that something was wrong. My mother handed her the chickens silently and disappeared into her bedroom to change her stained shirt.

"Where have you been?" Cook asked.

"We went to the Compound. She said she wanted chicken for dinner, not lamb."

Cook peeled the plum and handed me the skin. I

loved the tart, almost bitter taste. "Who saw you?" she asked.

I shrugged. I didn't want to tell her about the Host.

"Anyone from the Ministry?"

I shook my head.

Cook put down her knife. "Thomas, you must be very careful."

"I'm always careful." I was a cautious boy. I didn't take unnecessary risks.

"That's not what I mean. I know you're careful. But sometimes things can happen that are out of your control. Do you understand what I'm saying?"

Cook had a real name, Adalia, but in our household she had always been called Cook. She was much more than a cook. She was a nursemaid, a teacher, a skilled herbalist, and a surrogate grandmother. We knew each other so well that often we didn't even have to speak.

"Tonight, when the Seers come, don't try and eavesdrop."

"I don't. I never do," I said.

"I've got no time for lies, Thomas. Just do as I ask. Go to sleep tonight. Leave your parents to their business."

I gulped. I felt the tears coming again.

"Stop worrying," she said gruffly, picking up her

knife. She turned away from me. She had no desire to see me cry.

So I didn't worry. Not that night, when the house was filled with the booming voices of the Seers. Not the next morning, when my parents did not forecast each other's days at the breakfast table. Not even when they told me they would not be bringing me to the Ministry for my morning read.

"It's such a beautiful day, T," my father said. "Why don't you go pick us some blackberries?"

My mother rummaged around in the cabinet under the sink. "Here," she said, handing me a wooden pail. "I want to see that halfway filled." She thought about it a moment and added, "All the way filled would be even better."

"Can I go to our secret patch?" I asked. It was quite a distance, on the other side of the lake. "Please," I begged.

My father studied me, his head cocked. I had never seen tenderness on his face before and had no idea what to make of it. To me it looked like he was about to be sick.

"I think that's a fine idea," he said, ruffling my hair.

Thrilled, I ran out of the house. I had never been allowed to go that far alone.

"I'll be here when you get back," my father yelled after me. There was a note of desperation in his voice that made me want to get away from him as fast as I could.

It was noon when I returned. I was so excited to show my parents my overflowing pail that I nearly tripped over my father, who was sprawled out on the kitchen floor, his limbs rigid, his lips the oddest shade of lavender.

Dead.

My mother lay near the sink, conscious but barely so. She couldn't speak. She could only watch me from beneath her swollen eyelids.

A butcher knife lay on the table, its blade gleaming with a gelatinous gold speckled substance. While I had been out picking berries, my parents had been flayed of their Seerskins. My father's was balled up on the counter. My mother's was curled up beside her, like a fetus.

I was a small eight-year-old, compact enough to fit in the kitchen sink, and so I crawled into it. I wrapped my arms around my knees and rocked back and forth in that cold bowl. It never occurred to me to get help. I was simply . . . *alone.*

Hours passed. The candles, strangely lit in the middle of the day, flickered wildly on the counter, their flames horizontal, bending as if under some great weight. Greedy fingers of fire danced across my father's Seerskin. If I had just reached out with one hand I could have swept it to the floor, saved it from burning. But I was gripped with fear; I forgot I could move. There was a hideous musicality accompanying all this, a rattling percussive thrum that my father's skin made just before it turned to ash.

When the linen curtains above the sink caught fire, I understood I was next. At first it smelled good, familiar and safe, like buttery pecans or the promise of a barbecue. I looked up, mesmerized by the orange glow.

Then I heard the sound of a buckboard. Cook: she had come back to rescue me. Like many of the ordinary people in Isaura, she had a bit of the gift in her. Enough to make her hunches reality more often than not. I felt her weathered and chapped hands plucking me out of the sink. I reached up, clasping her around the neck like a baby.

It was ironic that my parents' gift showed itself in me at this particular moment. Cook *was* coming, but she'd just started down the dirt road; she wasn't in the kitchen, not yet. When I reached up, I tugged on the curtains and pulled the fire down atop myself.

Cook burst through the door just as I was falling to the ground. The top layers of my skin hung from my face like a giant sheet of wax. Cook would tell me later that I had no idea my face was aflame. I was cupping my chin as if I had just vomited and was trying to get to the bathroom before it splattered all over the floor.

Frenzied, she tried to take everything in at once: me on fire, my mother and father on the floor. My mother managed to croak one word, a command, "Thomas," which set Cook in motion. She ran to my side and put the fire out with a dish towel before it could spread. She applied pressure to my arms, my legs, and my torso—the places where I hadn't been burned.

"Go to sleep; that's a good boy. *Sleep.*"

An accommodating child, cradled in the arms of Cook, I fell away.

Days passed. I didn't know how many. I drifted in and out of consciousness. Cook was always at my side, changing the poultices on my face, feeding me a watery broth through a straw. She talked in a comforting, steady stream. She told me now was the time to be brave.

Every hour she gave me two teaspoons of an elixir made of wolfsbane and belladonna that kept me in a woozy, drugged state. A stranger named pain had moved into the house that was my body. It whispered that it had come to live with me forever. Nights were the worst, never ending and dark. I panted and hyperventilated my way through them. I flailed my arms and legs about; often I screamed.

Cook said, "If your body is a house, there must be rooms. Show pain into the parlor and then lock the door so it can't get out."

"Baby," my mother said when I opened my eyes a week later.

I looked around to see what newborn my mother was addressing. But the only new person in the room was her. A skinless mother, bizarrely dull to my eyes, like an old bolt or a piece of tarnished silver.

"Where have you been?" I asked. It came out like, "Ooo ah oo be?" but she understood what I meant.

She knelt down by my bed. "Right here."

"No. Cook's been here, not you," I said.

"I have too," she said softly.

"Then why haven't I seen you?"

"I've been—" She broke off.

"I thought you were dead," I said.

Her eyes pooled up with guilt. I could see that she didn't know where to touch me. She awkwardly took my hand, which was swaddled in bandages. It was burned too, but nowhere nearly as badly as my face. Still, I screamed and Cook came running.

"Leave us," my mother told her.

Cook slowly backed out of the room.

"I'm sorry I haven't come sooner," my mother said. "It's been hard for me to adjust to life without my Seerskin."

Her eyes searched my face. She was trying to find some safe place to rest her gaze. Somewhere not charred and seeping.

"Why would somebody do this?" I cried.

I was aware that neither of us was speaking of my father—of the fact that he was gone.

"The Ministry," she mumbled.

"Did they catch the person?" I interrupted her.

She shook her head. "No, no," she said. "You don't understand. They're not looking. They're doing nothing. They won't help. There's no place for us here anymore."

"Because you were skinned? That's not your fault!"

My mother touched my foot tenderly. "You don't belong here. None of us do. Not your father, not me, not you."

"Serena," Cook called out from the parlor.

"I said leave us alone, Adalia."

She turned back to me. "The Ministry," she continued.

"I don't understand. Why aren't they helping?" I sobbed.

My mother's eyes turned cold. "Listen to me, Thomas. This is their fault. You here. Like this . . . ." Her voice faltered, and I was filled with self-loathing. She was repulsed. She couldn't stand the sight of me, her ruined, burned boy.

Their fault? She was making no sense.

"You're saying they did this. The Ministry skinned you?" I asked.

Her eyes blinked rapidly, but she didn't deny it.

"But that's impossible. The Ministry was created to protect the Seers, not destroy them."

"Nothing's impossible," she said sadly. "I know that now."

Suddenly we heard a knock on Cook's front door. Through the parlor window we saw a flash of bright blue robe.

"Otak," my mother groaned.

Otak, the High Seer of the Ministry. My mother's great-uncle as well. Many of the more powerful Seers were related.

Despite what my mother had just told me, I was overcome with relief. She had gone crazy, blaming the Ministry for taking her skin. Otak would protect my mother and me. He would find the people who did this to my parents.

"He'll help us," I told her.

Cook strode into the bedroom and kicked aside a threadbare rug that hid the door to the root cellar. She pushed my mother down the stairs.

"But he's come to help," I whispered.

"No, Thomas," said Cook.

She took three deep breaths, then toed the rug back into place. She put her finger to her lips, warning me to be quiet, and shut the bedroom door. A few seconds later I heard the creak of the front door opening.

"Where is she?" Otak asked.

"She's not here," said Cook.

"The boy?"

"He's not here either."

I was terrified that he'd find me. But I was even more terrified that he wouldn't.

"I'm here," I brayed softly. "In the bedroom."

A few seconds later the door opened and Otak looked at me in silence. My face was covered in bandages. Blood and pus leaked through the white gauze. The room smelled like a butcher's shop, but his features were perfectly composed.

"Where's your mother?" he asked.

"They took her Seerskin," I said. "She can't help the way she's acting. She's gone crazy!"

Otak didn't answer me. He wandered around the bedroom, picking up bottles of Cook's tinctures and studying the labels. I couldn't stand the silence.

"Please help us," I pleaded with him. "Help her."

"I can't help her unless you tell me where she is."

"In the root cellar. There's a door under the rug," I told him, and passed out.

That evening I woke and found myself alone in the room with Cook. I was frantic. "What happened? Where's my mother?"

"Otak brought her to the Ministry," said Cook.

I could tell by the look on Cook's face that she was terribly worried, but she was trying to hide it from me. She unwound the crusty bandages, her practiced hands going through the motions, but she was in a daze, her thoughts elsewhere. She sniffed the gauze and frowned. It smelled terrible, like the innards of a pig.

"She thinks the Ministry did this to her. But she's wrong. They'll catch the people who did this to my parents. They'll help us," I said.

Cook was silent a moment. "Things are not always as they seem, Thomas." She dipped a rag in warm water and dabbed at my chin.

I grabbed her wrist. "Stop talking in riddles."

Cook dropped the rag into the bowl and sat back in her chair. "Very well. Your parents were part of a movement of Seers who wanted to stop prophesizing."

"Prophesizing?" I said weakly.

"Telling the future," said Cook.

"My parents loved their jobs," I protested, but even as I said it, I knew it wasn't true.

"They did not love their gift," said Cook. "What do you think all those meetings were about at your house?"

I closed my eyes. "Dinner parties," I whispered.

"No," said Cook gently.

"But they would have known what would happen. They would have foreseen that somebody was coming to skin them. They would have foreseen this!" I pointed at my face.

"They didn't know what would happen to you or to them, Thomas. They didn't take you to the Ministry that morning, remember? They didn't read for each other either," said Cook.

I gasped. Suddenly I understood what I had done. My mother had been telling me the truth after all. My parents had been made an example of, punished for their traitorous thoughts, and I had told Otak where my mother was hiding. I cried out with shame.

"Don't blame yourself," said Cook. "She would have had to meet with them sooner or later. You just made it sooner."

She was right, of course, but I would never forgive myself.

That night I was shaken awake. I blinked rapidly, like an owl. It was my mother. Without her Seerskin she was so ordinary. It was hard for me to look at her.

"Wake up, Thomas. We have to leave."

"You're back," I cried. I didn't realize until that second that the Ministry could have done something far worse to her than take her skin.

She nodded. "Get up. You can walk. There's nothing wrong with your legs."

"Where are we going?"

"We're leaving Isaura," she said. Her lips worked silently for a moment. "We've been exiled."

"No," I wailed.

"Yes," she said.

"Just tell them you're sorry. Apologize," I begged her.

"I'm sorry; I can't do that."

"Please!"

"I have no choice," she said.

"They can't make us go. We'll hide. We'll go to the mountains. They won't find us."

She shook her head miserably. "There's no place for us here anymore. Don't make me say it again, Thomas. Get up. *Now.*"

"But Cook—" I began.

"Cook has new patients to attend to."

"She wouldn't let me go. I'm not well enough."

"She wants you to come with me."

"I don't believe you."

"That's too bad; nevertheless, you're coming," she said firmly, tugging the blanket off me.

"But I have to say goodbye," I cried. "I can't just leave!"

"She told me to give you this."

My mother pressed a book into my hand, my Barker's. Suddenly I knew I'd never see Cook again.

The Ministry had exiled us to Earth. Later I would consult Barker's and find that there was no record of anything like this ever happening: our family was the first to be banished from Isaura.

We went by way of horse and carriage. My mother whispered to a man whose voice I didn't recognize. We traveled deep into the woods, and to calm myself, I pretended we were taking a marvelous journey to the Northlands. *Marvelous.* A word from a life that was no longer mine. I tried not to touch my face, since it was streaked with pus and blood.

An hour later we climbed out of the carriage. As soon as our feet touched the ground, the driver left. I was too weak to walk, so my mother carried me through a tunnel of laurel. The tunnel's mouth was wide and got narrower as we walked farther in. It felt like we were being tele-scoped. At the end of the tunnel we either began to rise or fall; I couldn't tell which. Perhaps it didn't matter—per-haps rising and falling were the same thing. But gravity released its hold; we spun like dust motes through a cop-pery quilt of light and passed out of our reality and into another.

FOUR

BACK IN THE PRESENT, THE doorbell rings, startling us both.

"Yoo-hoo," a voice yodels. "I've brought breakfast. I'm letting myself in."

Huguette. My mother's most loyal client.

"We'll talk about this tonight," my mother says. She begins to cough and soon she's gasping for breath. She waves at me, gesturing for a Kleenex. I hold out the tissue box and she stares up at me with bleary eyes.

"Reschedule Huguette. This can't wait until tonight," I say.

"No, we need the money." She shakes her head at me and begins hacking again.

Huguette walks into the bedroom. Barely eight in the morning and she's dressed and fully made up as if she were going to the opera. Around her neck she wears a silk scarf, elegantly tied. Her face falls when she sees the tray on the bed.

"Oh, you've already had breakfast." She looks at the quiche she's brought sadly.

"But she's eaten none of it," I say, taking the dish out of her hands. "Heat her up a piece after your session."

Huguette nods and hands me the latest issue of *Car and Driver*. She always brings me something: a cupcake, a set of drawing pencils, Chapstick.

"Tell me, what young man does not lust after cars?" she asks, content that I will now go and leave her with my mother.

Despite the fact that I'm desperate to continue my conversation with my mother, my exchange with Huguette is artful, and we both enjoy it, for there is a secret, cruder conversation lurking beneath. *You again. Yes, I know you're guardian of this house. Here's my offering. Now get the hell out.*

Even though Huguette's gesture is largely self-serving, she's not unkind, nor is she altogether wrong. I do lust after motorized vehicles, just not ones with four wheels; motorcycles are my passion. Still, I like that she takes the time to think what a teenager like me would enjoy. I mean, she could try so hard to pretend I'm normal that she would give me *Maxim* or *Details*, the grotesque images of a life that will never be mine. I adore Huguette. She sees no need to make apologies to me for my life.

"I'm afraid I have nothing to offer you," my mother tells Huguette, flashing me a dirty look.

I haven't done the shopping yet—I've been too busy with finals. I know what she's thinking: she's stuck in the house and I get to go out in the world. *With my puckered face.* She seems to forget about that.

"I ate hours ago," says Huguette.

My mother glances at the clock. "Patrick will be waiting," she says.

I swig the last of my orange juice and stuff my leather gloves into the bowl of my motorcycle helmet, stalling.

"I'll be all right," my mother says, her voice softening. "You can leave."

Huguette dismisses me. "Go, be with your tribe."

My tribe. Right.

FIVE

MY MOTHER SOUGHT HELP FOR me immediately after we arrived in Peacedale, a small town in the smallest state in America. We would have a lot of adjustments to make. America was years ahead of Isaura: it had electricity, cell phones, computers, and highways.

Isaura was stuck in the horse-and-wagon days. This was deliberate. We could have gone America's way; we had been on that track. But after the Great War the Ministry had decided that technological innovation would be the end of our civilization. So we'd purposely never moved beyond candle power and outhouses. We did have running water, the Ministry's one concession to modernity.

We wandered the streets at midnight. My mother knew we couldn't afford to be seen in the day, not with me looking like a mummy and pus seeping out from beneath my bandages. She found the Valley Rehabilitation Center at 2:45 a.m. The doors were locked. She led me back into the woods and made me take a big swallow of Cook's elixir so I could sleep.

"Just a few more hours," she said.

The next morning she brought me back to the reha-bilitation center. They took one look at my third-degree burns and rushed me to the Edward F. Anderson Burn

Unit, where I would spend the next month. My mother was left to fill out the forms.

"Names?"

"Serena and Thomas Quicksilver."

My mother had decided she would change our last name. Maybe she thought somebody might come looking for us from Isaura. Or maybe this was part of forgetting, of moving into our new life.

"Address?"

She was tempted to tell them our address in Isaura but couldn't bring herself to say the words out loud; she must look forward, not backward. Temporarily stumped, she said nothing.

The woman at the desk looked her up and down impatiently. "Transient?"

"Yes," my mother said. She didn't know yet what *transient* meant here. Not just "traveling," "in between places," but "homeless bum."

"I take it you have no insurance, then?"

My mother bristled, hearing the woman incorrectly. "Of course I'll give you assurance. He's a good, obedient boy. He's very brave. He suffers pain stoically. He will give you no trouble."

The receptionist looked at her like she was crazy. She wrote in big block letters on the form, UNABLE TO PAY.

"That's not the truth. I have money." My mother stabbed the form with her index finger.

She was lying. She had nothing but what she was wearing and a satchel that contained a wheel of cheese, my Barker's, and a sketch of her and my father on their wedding day.

My mother left me at the burn center on a Monday and didn't return until Friday evening. During that time I thought I would die. Every morning I was given a morphine drip and I fell into a deep slumber, only to be wrenched awake when they were cleaning my wounds. They peeled me like a roasted pepper. I had a tube in my mouth and a smaller tube in my nose. They told me even the inside of my throat was burned.

I couldn't single out anybody's face, for the shifts changed often and time was either stretched out or abbreviated. An hour could last half a day or go by in three minutes. But their voices I could differentiate. There was one nurse I liked. She spoke to me tenderly, as if I were her child. If her voice could have had a color, it would have been molten orange. You may think this strange, that I found the color of fire soothing. But I had eaten fire; it had marked me as its own and we would be kin for life.

"How did it happen, Thomas?" the nurse with the orange voice asked.

"Candle. Curtains." Full sentences were beyond me.

"Somebody cared for you. Some sort of herbal poultice?"

"My mom." We had agreed I would say this.

"She did a good job; she kept the wounds clean. But I'm glad she brought you here."

I didn't answer, because she was peeling a long strip of skin off my cheek with a pair of tweezers.

"Just this last one," she promised. I trusted her and steeled myself. She was not like some of the other nurses, who would lie and tear off the skin without warning, thinking it was better to be surprised.

I knew what was coming next: the Xeroform, this cold yellow goop they spread on before the layers of gauze and Ace bandages. I loved this part. The ointment was cool and smelled like mints. The nurse's hands became Cook's hands applying the poultices, and my two worlds, Isaura and Earth, became one. Done with my torture for the day, I sank back into the arms of the morphine.

My mother told me she spent the first day trying to get a job. Anything: waitressing, working in a toy factory, cataloging books at the library. She had no references, no job experience, and was turned away everywhere. She did the same thing the next day. People were far less generous on Tuesday. She smelled. Her hair was uncombed, her clothes unkempt. She was thrown out of more than one place. On Wednesday she made the rounds once again, walking into every storefront, every bank and grocery store. On Thursday, desperate, with fifty-five cents to her name (that she had found in a phone booth), she went into a café and sat at the counter. Her feet hurt. The two men sitting to her left moved into a booth. She tried to smooth down her hair.

"What do you want, honey?" The waitress, a woman in her fifties who wore her pink uniform with panache, looked at her kindly and my mother didn't know what to make of it. This world was so different from her own. People showed their emotion all the time in America. She could see what people felt when they walked down the street, when they talked on the phone; it was even evident in the way they drove their cars. She found it exhausting.

"I have fifty-five cents," she said to the waitress, showing her the coins.

"You can stay here twenty minutes—half an hour, tops. I'm sorry, but you smell and it's bad for business. Fifty-five cents will buy you a cup of coffee and a pastrami sandwich," said the waitress.

My mother didn't know the cost of things yet, so she didn't know the waitress was doing her a favor. The food came quickly and my mother gobbled it down. When the waitress brought her a large glass of milk, then my mother understood she was being nice.

"Thank you," said my mother, touching her hand. The waitress flinched, unable to move as an invisible current of energy leapt between them and my mother received a vision of the waitress later that night opening the door to a middle-aged man.

"Tonight you will have a visitor. It's been twenty-two years since you've seen him," my mother told her.

The waitress, spooked, retracted her hand. "I think you'd better go."

My mother found a park and sat under a tree, far away from the small children and their mothers, their strollers, their bags of snacks and juice boxes. As soon as she sat, her grief began to rise, from her toes up through her body. The tears started slowly, just one creeping down her left cheek. A few minutes later she was weeping openly.

Her visions had returned. In this world she could see the future even without her Seerskin. Something must have happened when she passed through the portal. She had never considered that Isaurian magic might manifest itself differently here.

The following morning she went back to the café and again sat at the counter. The waitress walked up to her slowly. My mother was unfamiliar with the complex look on her face: gratitude, awe, and a tiny bit of fear.

"You have a gift," the waitress said.

"Some call it that," said my mother.

"There are people who would be interested in your gift and would pay well for it."

"I'd need a place to see them."

The waitress pointed to a table in the back. "You can work there. There's a shower in the back. Go get cleaned up. I'll make some calls."

My mother hesitated. "I don't know what to charge. I don't know how to attach value to this thing . . . what I can do."

She looked at the waitress—at her shiny face, her perfectly coiffed hair. Pinned to the woman's uniform was a name tag that read *Huguette*.

Huguette didn't hesitate. "One hundred dollars," she said.

By Friday evening, when my mother returned to the burn unit, she had told twenty-two fortunes, had put a security deposit down on an apartment, and had five hundred dollars in cash. She marched up to the receptionist's desk.

"My first payment," she told the woman, slapping

the money down in front of her. The woman looked at her suspiciously.

"I thought you said you were a transient."

By this time my mother knew that *transient* was an insult.

"You'll get five hundred dollars a week until my bill is paid off."

It was May when I had my first graft. In June my mother was told she could take me home to rest, but she would need to bring me back in September for another series of grafts.

My mother came to pick me up from the hospital in a Chevy Impala. I hadn't seen, never mind ridden in, an automobile before. I couldn't believe that people lived like this, with so many conveniences.

I rolled down the window. The air smelled of wood smoke. I gulped in the familiar scent like oxygen. I saw children playing ball in the streets and mothers hanging up laundry in their backyards. All of these people with their easy, taken-for-granted lives. I missed Isaura, I missed Cook, and I missed my father most of all.

"I thought you'd like the car, Thomas," my mother said. "Everyone has them here."

"I hate it." I was lying, of course. I was fascinated by the car.

I had been waiting to leave the hospital for so long, but now that the day was here, I couldn't wait for it to be over. The sight of my mother's worn face, her eagerness to have me home, and her excitement for us to start our new life sickened me. Didn't she miss Isaura? Didn't she hate it here, on the world to which we had been banished?

"Stop looking at me," I cried.

My mother sat quietly, absorbing my rage. "We have to make the best of it, Thomas. This is our life now. This is where we live."

"I'll never get used to it," I said.

My mother reached out for me and I flinched, trying to get as far away from her as I could. Then I caught a glimpse of myself in the passenger-side mirror. My face was no longer oozing: instead it was a patchwork of purplish squares, skin harvested from my stomach. I wept hard and noisily, my rib cage heaving up and down. My mother kept driving, but she reached out and covered my hand with hers.

"I know it seems that way now," she said.

Now she began to cry. I made myself watch her. What a funny thing, crying. The way her shoulders jerked up and down, how she let the tears stream down her neck and wet her shirt collar.

"Stop it," I finally said.

She nodded, but it took her a few minutes to collect herself. It was my first experience with telling my mother what to do. It frightened me, this power.

"I like the car," I admitted. "How did you get it?" I ran my hands over the red vinyl seats.

"I bought it."

"But how did you pay for it?"

"Doing readings."

I stared at her in shock. "But you don't have your Seerskin."

"That's right—I don't have my Seerskin," she repeated.

"Then how can you see the future?"

My mother pounded the steering wheel with her fists. "You think I know?" she cried.

The car swerved to the left and I slid into my mother. I quickly scuttled back to my side of the seat—I didn't want to touch her. Because of her rebellion, my father was dead and we had been exiled to America. But apparently it had all been for nothing, because here she was, still getting visions, even without her skin!

"But Barker's," I said.

"Damn Barker's!" she shouted. "The magic works differently here, Thomas."

A car whizzed by and my mother winced. I thought

she was reacting to the roar of the engine—America was so loud. I didn't know she was flinching because she had just received a vision that the driver would run a red light at the next cross section and hit a dog. What my mother hadn't told me yet was that her ability to see into the future had intensified without the protection of her Seerskin. She no longer had to be touching somebody to see their future. In Isaura a skinless Seer would go mad from the loss of visions. Here in this world, a skinless Seer would go mad from too many visions. My mother would hide this from me for years.

"I'm afraid," I whispered.

My mother pulled the car over to the side of the road. I was quaking, cramming myself into the space in front of the passenger seat. She got out, walked around the car, opened my door, and gathered me up. She carried me into the shade of a giant beech tree.

"It's all right, baby. It's all right," she crooned.

It was four in the afternoon. It was a busy road, a main thoroughfare. At this time of the day the traffic was largely made up of women shuttling their children from school to soccer, from violin lessons to the dentist. I had my back to the road and to them must have looked like a perfectly normal boy.

These women, these kind women, nodded to my

mother as they drove by, the way mothers acknowledged other mothers when their children threw tantrums in the stores, or hurled their shoes into a pond, or threw up after eating too much candy. We were just like them, just another mother and child having a rocky moment. Until I turned around and they saw my face.

My mother had rented the upstairs of a two-family home in Rockridge: not the best of neighborhoods, but not the worst.

"Mums." She pointed to the two pots that she'd placed on either side of our front door.

I shrugged; I was too young to comprehend the effort she'd put into making that apartment presentable. Suddenly the door opposite ours flew open with great force. I took an involuntary step backward.

"Whoa!" said a redheaded woman, catching sight of me. Then, a long drawn-out "Whoa" again.

She tried to look at me without flinching. She couldn't do it. Her eyes slid off mine and darted around my face like dragonflies looking for a safe place to land. Eventually she focused on a spot by my temple.

I had been forewarned that this would happen. The staring, the looking away, the coming back for more. I felt a crushing loneliness; even at that young age I knew I would always be alone, the old Thomas looking out from the new Thomas's monstrous face.

My mother put her hand on my shoulder protectively. "Marla, this is my son, Thomas."

"Your son? I didn't know you had a son."

My mother unlocked the door and pushed me ahead of her onto the stairs. The screen door latched behind us. Marla pressed her face to the mesh. "How'd he get burned?"

My mother didn't answer.

"Hey, I asked you a question. How'd he get burned?"

"That's none of your business," my mother said.

Marla let out a large "humph."

My mother hesitated, her fingers twitching.

"Hey, little man. Head up. You don't look so bad," Marla called out to me.

I spun around. Any kind thing said by someone belonging to the normal world would make me beholden to them; it would be this way for many years. I gave Marla a little wave and my mother marched me up the stairs.

The next afternoon I overheard Marla talking to her boyfriend in the backyard.

"The kid's a freak. Wait till you see him. His face looks like uncooked sausage."

Grown-ups lied. They lied all the time.

I had endured only one out of what would be five skin grafts. The first week I was home I missed the rehabilitation center terribly. I had gotten close to many of the nurses in the burn unit, in particular one named Clara Graves—she of the molten orange voice. She had a crooked fang tooth and long blond hair and she smelled of gardenias. Often she would bring me gifts: yo-yos, something called an Etch A Sketch, and once a packet of Twinkies. I couldn't bring myself to eat them. They looked too perfect—twin loaves of yellow sponge cake. I waited until she left and threw them out.

One day the doorbell rang.

"Thomas!" my mother called.

I ran to the top of the stairs. At first I didn't recognize Clara: she was out of her hospital greens and her hair was loose instead of pulled back into a ponytail. She waved gaily. Attached to her hand was a boy. Did she know I had thrown away the Twinkies? Had she come to yell at me?

"Are you up for some company?" Clara asked.

I wasn't sure. I wanted to see Clara but was nervous about the boy.

"Okay," I said.

The boy ran up the stairs first. He was shorter than me but stronger and stockier. His hair was a silvery brown and cut choppily all over his head so that it stood up. He plowed into me like a little bull.

"I'm seven and three-quarters," he crowed.

I fell to the ground.

"Patrick Edward Graves!" Clara shouted.

Patrick got up, slapping his jeans with his hands. "Sorry." He stood very close to me and examined my face.

"Does it hurt?"

"Not right now."

"It looks like Silly Putty."

"Yup," I said, for this was the truth and Patrick was the first one to speak it.

From that moment on we were inseparable.

Our first two years were relatively happy ones. My mother worked hard to shield me from her pain, and she *was* in pain without her Seerskin, bodily and emotional anguish. I loved her for pretending. For giving me those years of boyhood, for they were all I was going to get.

"We're alive, Thomas," my mother would say to me while we chopped vegetables for dinner and listened to the radio. Sometimes the songs would make her sad. Then I knew she was missing my father. Other times they'd make her want to dance. She'd grab me and swing me wildly around the kitchen.

"What's happened to you?" I asked, for in Isaura she had paid no attention to me. None of the parents paid any attention to their children in Isaura.

"This world," she said. "That's what happened to me. And to you too. Don't you feel it?"

I shrugged, unsure.

"We're living in a world that doesn't know its future. So there's wonder and mystery, pain and joy," she said.

Pain, I understood. Joy was new to me.

She took me to movies, to concerts, to museums and plays. My favorite times were weekends. We'd just get in the car and go. No destination, just a glove compartment full of maps, a jug of Kool-Aid, and a box of Hostess cupcakes. We'd drive at night. Shadows were my friends. The smells were best then too, as if they sensed they were in danger of disappearing forever. The tar beneath our wheels still held the heat of the day and the vinyl backseats smelled faintly of old tobacco. I'd navigate, my small body hunched over in the seat, reading the map by penlight. *Go right, no, left!*

Those weekends were wonderful, until we stopped

for gas and the moment came for me to leave the front seat to buy chewing gum or use the bathroom. That meant leaving the secure world of me and my mother and entering a world in which I had no companions. The twenty feet to the service station store felt like twenty miles. By the time I got back to the car, I was straitjacketed in shame.

When I turned eleven, everything abruptly changed. My mother could no longer hide what was happening from me. She began to receive visions at all times of the night and day. She couldn't be within twenty feet of the door or she was assaulted by the future. She saw everything that would befall everybody with no discrimination. Random people: the kid riding by on his bike, the teenager throwing the newspaper, every passenger of every car. She even saw the futures of animals—moles, gophers, cats, dogs, doves, owls—for they had futures just as we did, only less complicated. Their concerns and dilemmas? Would they get a scratch behind the ears or nothing? Would their owners come home in time to let them out or would they piddle on the floor? My mother could see the answers to all these questions, and so she stayed in the back of the house, buffered by the thick plaster walls and by me.

SIX

I DRIVE THROUGH THE STREETS unsteadily that morning, weaving my motorcycle in and out of traffic. I pull up in front of Patrick's, my tires squealing. He's sitting on the front steps in his usual uniform, a white T-shirt and camouflage pants. He's still shorter than me by about three inches, maybe five-ten, but we have completely different body types. I'm tall and what you would call rangy. John, my occupational therapist, tells me that well-developed shoulders will shift attention away from my face. I like to believe his lies.

Patrick is interested in nothing but bulk. He's a wrestler, 168 pounds. He still wears his hair the same way he did when he was seven: in a buzz cut. He's an awesome drummer and my best friend, even after all these years.

He raises his eyebrows at me. "You're late."

"Thanks for the news flash," I say, and toss him my extra helmet.

I have ridden Patrick to school on the back of my motorcycle every day for the last year, since I got my license. If you were to ask him why he prefers to be a passenger on my bike rather than drive his own car, I'm not sure what he'd say. Probably something about getting to school faster, running red lights, that sort of thing. For me it's one word—freedom. From the neck down I have a perfectly normal body, and when I'm on my motorcycle, nobody knows about my face. I'm just another anonymous human being, a pair of legs and boots, a torso and tanned forearms.

Patrick tosses the helmet back to me as a car pulls up to the curb. Meg Greer—Patrick's new girlfriend of one week—sits behind the wheel of an Outback.

"Oh," I say.

"Hi, Tom," says Meg.

Nobody who knows me ever calls me Tom.

"He prefers Thomas," says Patrick.

"Thomas, then," says Meg. She's Irish. Lots of freckles, a nimbus of curly black hair, pale skin. She isn't being disingenuous. She's making an effort because I'm Patrick's best friend, but for some reason this annoys me.

"Can I get a ride after school?" Patrick asks, sliding into the passenger seat of Meg's car. He's trying to make it up to me.

I feel Meg's eyes on me even through my helmet. She can't help staring. I have a face that can give life. It reminds people of how fortunate they are. They can riff off my ugliness back into their own humanity. In other words, I startle them right back into their own skins.

I'm angry. Patrick should have called and told me not to come. I climb off the bike, open the pannier, and jam in the extra helmet. I slam the lid shut. "What time?"

"Five? After practice?" he says.

I shake my head. "Sorry."

"I'll pick you up," says Meg to Patrick.

"You do that," I say, starting the bike.

SEVEN

THE DAY GOES STEADILY DOWNHILL from there. I can't stop thinking about my mother. I almost leave, but I haven't cut even one class in all three years of high school.

"Tunisia, Mr. Quicksilver. Would you do us the honor of locating it?"

Mr. Laird, my history teacher, stands at the front of the classroom, the map of the world (well, this world, anyway) to his left, a pointer in his right. It's our last week of classes before summer break, and Mr. Laird is unhappy in the way many high school teachers are: overworked, underpaid, and underappreciated. I've made the mistake of not turning in most of my homework assignments but still acing my exams. He stabs the pointer in my general direction, which means I am to come to him.

"Puckkkkerrrr . . ." somebody hisses from the front of the classroom.

Mr. Laird grimaces but says nothing. I can't read his face. I don't think he's upset on my behalf but on his own—that he has to continually endure these interruptions.

As I make my way to the front of the class, I accidentally brush the shoulder of Susie Egan. She recoils and then tries to hide it by dropping her pencil on the floor and bending to pick it up. I can smell her hair. She uses the same shampoo as me. This unexpected jolt of intimacy startles me. Unnerved and electrified, I stumble up the aisle. I quickly find Tunisia on the map and turn to go back to my seat.

"Not so fast, Mr. Quicksilver," says Mr. Laird.

I hate it when teachers call you "Mr."

"The motto of Florida?" he queries me.

"In God we trust," I answer.

"Alaska?"

Ah, so this is the game. Public humiliation. "North to the future," I say.

"Iowa?"

"Our liberties we prize and our rights we will maintain."

Mr. Laird is getting angry that he can't trip me up. I can't get the scent of Susie's shampoo out of my mind, or the fact that she's wearing white pants.

"Annapurna? Where is it?"

"Nepal, 26,041 feet." He should know better than to ask me these sorts of questions. I have a near-photographic memory.

Susie Egan is wearing white pants.

I have a hunch. Public humiliation is indeed coming, but not to me.

"Elbrus?" Mr. Laird asks.

"Russia, 18,841 feet." I have to get back to my seat and warn her. The class is snickering. This could go on forever.

"Jungfrau?" I fire back at him.

Mr. Laird glares at me. I'm questioning *him*?

"Switzerland, 13,642 feet," I answer before he has a chance to. "Jaya?" I demand.

"Watch it, Quicksilver," Mr. Laird warns.

"Jaya?" I repeat. "How high?"

"In your seat," Mr. Laird roars.

The classroom is silent. I walk back to my desk and sit down. "New Guinea, 16,500 feet," I whisper. Two minutes later I try and pass Susie Egan a note. She won't accept it. She looks at it with disgust, as if I have attempted to give her a horse turd.

Unfortunately, Mr. Laird sees the note too. "Bring it up here," he barks.

I have no choice.

Mr. Laird opens the note and reads it, his lips twitching, then he folds it up into fours and hands it back to me. He nods and gestures with his head toward Susie. So my note goes back to Susie Egan, who reads it quickly while the entire class watches. She asks to be excused.

And what does my note say? Well, that's private. Let's just say those white pants would have been ruined had she stayed in her seat a few moments longer.

It isn't the first time I've had a hunch. I often have them: many times they are wrong; some of the time they are accurate. I knew this isn't unusual, given that I come from a place where 10 percent of the population is Seers. There's a big difference between having the occasional hunch and being a Seer, however. I don't read anything into my hunches; I suspect they are nothing more than neural misfirings.

But back to Susie Egan. Some would say she deserves it. What sixteen-year-old girl dares to tempt fate by wearing white pants a day before her period is due? A girl like Susie Egan, of course, to whom everything has always come easy. But I have a responsibility.

Besides, I know about such things as periods. I'm not squeamish. I don't have the kind of life that affords me time or room for being squeamish. I do, however, know about embarrassment. And as much as I may hate Susie Egan for being repulsed by me, neither do I wish on her humiliation.

EIGHT

I STOP AT MCDONALD'S AFTER school. I have a battered copy of Joseph Conrad's *Heart of Darkness* in my hand. I never go anywhere without a book. That way I'm never alone.

There are two kids in front of me in line.

"Crispy," one of them says on seeing me. He punches his buddy on the shoulder and giggles nervously. "You want fries with that?"

The other one, whose face is covered with acne, replies, "I'd like my burger well done, sir."

"Let my people go," I say.

They look at me with startled faces. What? The creature speaks?

I sigh. "The burning bush? The Red Sea parting?"

Dolts. The light slowly creeps back into their faces as if I've released them from a burden they no longer have to carry. Funny, this guy is funny? Of course they are immensely grateful, but they have no idea for what. They know only that something overly swollen has been punctured and now it's safe to breathe.

"You're all right, man," the acned one says. He looks at me good-deedishly, as if I've been waiting all these years for him to bestow on me his blessing. I feel bad for him. He has angry red boils scattered over his cheeks, miniature mountains of pus lodged in the corners of his nose and lips. I know something he doesn't: the closer their experience is to mine, the meaner they get. Me and this zitty kid are family. Of course I could never suggest that. He would kill me. I shrug and step out of line. I no longer have an appetite.

When I was young, I was ugly, but I still had youth on my side: my limbs were plump and rounded; I had baby teeth like everyone else. I was precocious and brave, wise beyond my years. I was the sad, cute burned boy. Those years are gone. Now, in place of the compassion, I see mostly revulsion and fear. A burned boy grows up into a burned teenager with size-twelve feet. He does not get more endearing. He simply takes up more space.

NINE

W HEN I GET HOME, JOE COSTANZA, one of my
mother's regulars, is leaving. We meet on the stairs. He
looks shaken. I know he's been asking my mother the big
question: time of death. Only he didn't want the information for himself, but for his eight-year-old daughter,
Audrey, who's been in and out of the hospital with some
illness they haven't been able to diagnose yet.

My mother tried to dissuade him. For weeks she put
him off, telling him no .parent should be privy to this
data. I guess he finally wore her down.

"Hey, Sport," he says to me in a weak voice.

"Hi, Mr. Costanza."

"I'm afraid our session took it out of your mother.
It's good you're home," he says.

I always wonder what my mother's clients make of
her bedridden status. Does it make them uncomfortable
to have some woman in a nightgown telling their fortunes, or does it somehow add to the authenticity of
the experience?

"She's been under the weather," I say. That's an under-
statement, but I know a minimizing of the situation is
required.

He grips my shoulder once tightly and turns to go.

He swivels around when he reaches the bottom stair. "She was right. I shouldn't have asked."

"Probably." What else can I say to him?

"I just—when do I tell my wife?" he asks me.

"Never!" I'm shocked that he's even contemplating this. "You asked the question. It's your responsibility to bear the answer."

"You're right; you're right, of course," he says, his face knotted in pain. "But how do *I* bear it?"

"You just do," I say.

TEN

"THOMAS!" MY MOTHER HOLLERS WHEN I get upstairs.

Now that she's ready to talk, I'm not. I stand in the kitchen ignoring her. After all these years, just like that, she tells me I have to go back to Isaura?

I pound down two Dr. Peppers and pick up the phone to call Patrick. Then I remember it's Friday night: he's out with Meg. I feel sorry for myself for about half a minute— oh, poor me, the rest of the world out on a Friday night, that kind of sorry-ass feeling that I rarely indulge—then I get up and leave. I have to get out, away from my mother and our insane past.

There are many trails in the woods behind my house and I know them all. I don't need a flashlight, nor do I need to drop any crumbs. Even if I wandered three miles into that thick, dense woodland, I could find my way out. But I'm not alone tonight.

The sight of the couple enrages me at first. These are my woods. Everybody else has the entire world.

"Here. Sit," the girl says, patting the plaid blanket.

She lies back, arranging her hair so that it streams out from her head in ribbons. She rolls up her shirt, exposing her stomach. Her belly is taut and tanned.

"You can touch me," she says to the boy.

He hesitates.

"I'm not a slut," she says, sitting up on her elbows.

He doesn't need a second invitation. His hand descends and he lays his palm flat on her stomach. I imagine the heat of her skin. It would be like holding a little rabbit.

Everything is connected. You can't touch one thing without sensing the presence of another; it's simply not possible.

She rolls her shirt up to her clavicle. Suddenly, with a sigh of impatience, she sits up, unhooks her bra, and drops it to the ground. Her breasts are perfect, silvered by the moon. I've never seen real breasts before. For the first time in my life I forget I'm burned, and I'm just a boy and there is a girl and some invisible cord connects us.

But there's also another boy and it isn't me, and it's he who gets to touch her, he who gets to make her gasp.

I need to leave before I do something I'll regret, like stay longer than I should. Quietly, as has become my way in this world, I go.

ELEVEN

"WHERE HAVE YOU BEEN?" MY mother asks.

"Out," I say.

My mother stiffens. "Traipsing around town with your friends when I've just told you I'm going to drop dead any day!"

I stare at her emptily. "I don't have any friends," I say softly.

Slowly the anger drains from her face. The cynic in me whispers that she can't afford to stay mad at me for long—I'm the one who makes sure our electricity doesn't get shut off.

"That's not true. Stop exaggerating. You have friends," she snaps.

I'm breaking our unspoken agreement. Because my mother has been sick, part of what's required of me is a certain amount of dishonesty, or withholding of information. She's not strong enough for me to add the burden of my suffering to her own, and up until this moment I've abided by this rule. Suddenly, though, I need her to know who I am.

"You don't care about me. You left me here alone," she sobs.

Her emotional theatrics are exhausting. I drop down on the bed. I feel like I did just after I got my first skin graft. I remember lying on a gurney in the recovery room. My morphine had run out and the nursing staff hadn't noticed. I was an eight-year-old boy dog-paddling in the middle of the ocean, waiting for the next giant wave of pain to pin me to the seafloor.

My mother's tears dry up and she finally notices me, as if I've appeared by some sleight of hand. For a second the mother who would be rightly mine had I not been burned, had her Seerskin not been flayed, looks benevolently at me.

"I miss Dad," I say.

The corners of her mouth pleat in sympathy. "I miss him too."

She reaches over and strokes my hair. I've been touched so few times in my life by anyone other than surgeons and nurses that I'm starved. I make the mistake of scooting up closer and her face clouds with despair.

"What am I going to do?" she moans. Her head lolls back on the pillow and my thirty seconds of being a kid are over.

I sigh. "First, you can stop being so melodramatic," I say, sitting up. "I'll go."

"You will?" she says, propping herself up on her elbows.

"Yes, but you need to give me some answers first."

"Anything," she says.

"Well . . . won't they be expecting me? I mean, they can see the future; they'll know I'm coming."

"I don't think so. They'd have to be touching you to read your future. Plus Otak is related to us by blood, so he won't be able to forecast anything about you, and he's one of the few Seers I know of who would be strong enough to see something like this." She frowns. "But there's no way to know for certain until you get there."

I pause, absorbing this, and something else nags at

me. "How do you know your Seerskin is still there?" I ask.

"Of course it's there," she whispers, looking stricken. "Seerskins are valuable. The Ministry would never destroy it."

"But how do you know?" I press her. "How can you be so sure?"

She shakes her head. "I just am."

Her eyes flitter away from me. The light from the lamp shines through her ears and for a moment I see the girl that she once was.

"You know because you can sense it?" I ask her gently.

She nods. "*Yes.* That's it. It's like it's out there, a piece of me, and it's been waiting all these years for someone to rescue it and bring it home."

Tears spring suddenly to my eyes and I turn away, not wanting her to see them. I see myself moments before the fire, my arms wrapped around my knees, rocking.

"All right," I say briskly, trying to ward off this image. "How do I get there?"

She exhales loudly. "I'm afraid you'll have to be recruited."

"Recruited? Like the Changed?" I ask.

"Like the Changed," she repeats.

I stare at her incredulously. "But what about the portal? I'll just go back there. I'll sneak through," I say.

She shakes her head. "It's not there anymore. I had Huguette check."

"You told Huguette? About *us*?"

My mother looks at me defiantly. Two bright circles of red stain her cheeks. "I had to. Who's going to help me when you're gone? You can't expect me to manage on my own."

"You swore," I say. "*We* swore not to tell anyone."

"That was before I foresaw my death." My mother gives me a weak smile. "Bet your Barker's had nothing about this in it."

"I haven't seen my Barker's in years," I snap.

She leans over and opens her bedside table drawer. "Here," she says, handing me the brown book. Nostalgia threads through me at the sight of it, not altogether unpleasant, but the book also makes me feel strangely claustrophobic, as if someone has just locked me in a tiny room. I push it away. She places it on the bed between us.

"There's a map of the Ministry in there. It'll help you remember," she says.

"Remember what?" I say, irritated. As if I need any help remembering.

My mother hesitates. "How it was," she says. "It wasn't all bad. We were happy there once."

The last thing I want to hear is that we were happy in Isaura. I get up from the bed and glare at her. "So there's no portal."

"There's a portal. You just need somebody to take you there. Thomas, believe me, I've thought this through. The only way for you to get back to Isaura is to go back as one of the Changed. And to do that you must convince a Recruiter that you're a qualified candidate. That means you have to pretend you're suicidal. That things are so bad you want out."

I have a sudden vision of a storefront with a poster in the front window. *We want you.* And a long line of freaks from the circus: hollow man, seal girl, and me.

"The Recruiters are here in Peacedale?"

I fight down my nausea. The thought sickens me. Now that we live on Earth, the Recruiters seem like predators. Back in Isaura, when we depended on the Changed for our food, our clean linens, and our cobbled streets, those who recruited them were heroes.

"Yes. They're many places in America. They pose as psychiatrists. You remember Dr. Caro at the rehabilitation center?" she says.

Dr. Caro: I had always hated the guy, just on principle.

He was loud and took up every speck of oxygen in the room and he was always after me to get evaluated. The last thing I wanted to do was tell some stranger I had been nicknamed Pucker.

"But won't he know? Won't he be able to tell I'm Isaurian?" I ask.

"No. Not if you're careful. Recruiters aren't Seers. He can't read you. But the Maker *is* a Seer, and that's a problem."

I stare at my mother, bewildered.

"Once you get to Isaura, you'll be brought to the Maker. She'll have to go back into your past," she says.

"But if she sees my past, she'll know I'm your son," I say.

"Yes," says my mother. "So you'll have to be very careful about letting her in. You must shield your memory from her. You'll need to give her details. But do not give her the big picture. Do not show her your father and me."

"How am I supposed to do that?" I cry. Even now, so many years later, whenever I think of that day, all I can see is my father lying on the floor, dead, his Seerskin balled up on the counter.

"Just focus on colors," my mother says. "Smells. Textures. The curtains were yellow, remember? The kitchen smelled of cobbler. That'll be enough for the Maker to work with."

"I can't," I whimper.

"You can," says my mother sharply. "You must control your inner gaze. Just remember yourself sitting in the sink. Show her the curtains falling on top of you."

"Then what?"

"Then she'll make it so that the fire never happened. Your scars will disappear. Your face will be healed," my mother says.

My mouth drops open in shock. How had I never thought of this? My hands rise to my face, to the ribbons of scar tissue. I feel like I've just been told that it's been in my power the whole time to reverse my destiny. That with one savage tug I could have just peeled off my fate.

My mother takes my hands and places them back in my lap. "You'll have the face you were meant to have had the fire not happened. But it's only temporary, Thomas. Once you come back, the Maker's magic will fall apart. Do you understand?" she asks.

I don't answer her.

"Do you understand, Thomas?" my mother asks again, gently tilting my chin upward, forcing me to look at her.

I nod dully.

"Tell me what I just said."

"When I come back, I'll be Pucker again."

Her eyes bat involuntarily as if I've struck her, and I wrench my face out of her hand. Adrenaline surges through me. I have the sudden need to destroy something. I grab a figurine of a rabbit, a gift from one of her clients.

"Not that!" my mother shrieks.

"It's from the freaking Hallmark store!" But I obey her. I put it back on the bureau and grab a pillow. I ram my fist into it again and again.

"I'm sorry. Thomas. Please, stop!"

"Do you have any idea what you're asking of me?" I scream.

"I'd go myself if I could," she moans. "I swear I would."

She erupts into another coughing fit. This one's really bad, brought on by me, no doubt. She's not faking it.

"It's like somebody's shredding my bones," she sobs.

"Stop talking," I tell her. "Just stop it. Conserve your strength. You're making it worse."

After a bit, when the pain has subsided and she's caught her breath, she touches my cheek softly. "It's horribly unfair. It's too much to ask of you, but I don't have a choice," she says.

And here, finally, is the truth. It sits in the room with us like a long-lost relative just come back from a war.

TWELVE

I DON'T SLEEP AT ALL that night. I sit in the kitchen and watch the clock until it's morning; then I call Patrick. His mother answers the phone.

"He's in the bathroom, sweetie; I'll have him call you right back."

Clara Graves is a second mother to me. There's nobody who knows more about what it's like to be a burn victim than she does.

"That's all right. Just give him a message. Tell him we're going to breakfast this morning. My treat."

There's a pause. "Everything okay?" she asks.

"Yeah, fine." It isn't fine; it's so far from fine. I have the sudden urge to confess everything. Where we come from, what I am about to do.

I want to be little again. I want Clara to invite me for

a sleepover. She fed us chocolate milk and Three Musketeers bars for dinner.

"Is it Meg?" she asks softly. "I don't think he's that serious about her."

I don't answer. My throat feels like it's wadded up with cotton.

"Your Meg will come," she says, and much to my surprise, her voice is all rough and pebbly. "I promise, Tommy."

Oh, how I love her for lying.

"Yeah, sure," I say. "Tell Patrick I'll be there in half an hour."

THIRTEEN

YE OLD EGG SHOPPE IS PACKED. There are no seats, but I know the password.

"Huguette," I say, and they find a place for us at the counter. I look at the booth in the back where my mother told her first fortunes in this world: where she made her first friend. I wonder—will I be given a password to get back to Isaura?

Patrick and I order. Eggs and ham on an English

muffin for him, French toast for me, even though I know I won't eat. I sip my coffee nervously. It's my fourth cup.

"So, what's up?" asks Patrick, biting into his breakfast sandwich.

"I'm thinking about going away for part of the summer," I say.

"Why?" he asks, his mouth crammed full. "It's our last summer before senior year. Last summer of freedom. This fall's gonna suck, man."

"It's a favor for my mother. A family obligation."

"I thought you didn't have any family: it was just you and your mom."

"I never told you about my aunt who lives in California?"

Patrick scowls and pops a piece of my French toast into his mouth. "I hate this fake maple syrup crap. And you're a pathetic liar, Quicksilver."

"I'm not lying," I say.

Patrick chews thoughtfully. "So this 'aunt' of yours? What's her name?"

"Betty."

"Okay," he says. "Auntie Betty. And what are you going to do at Auntie Betty's house?"

I shrug. "Hang out. Go to Disneyland."

"Mm-hmm," he says. "And just where does Auntie Betty live?"

"California. I told you."

"Where in California?"

"Oh. Oakland."

"Disneyland's in southern California, pal," Patrick says, sopping up his egg yolks with a heel of bread.

I sigh. "Patrick—"

He waves his hand at me. "Just don't lie to me, Thomas. We've been through too much."

I don't say anything. He's right, of course. I slide my plate across the counter. A peace offering. He grunts his thanks and digs in. I signal the counterman for more coffee. Patrick puts his hand over my mug.

"Don't you think you've had enough?" he asks, eyeing my leg, which has been jittering up and down the entire time we've been there. "How long have you been up, anyway?"

"Too long," I say. "All night."

Patrick shakes his head. "Oakland's no Peacedale. You better be careful. Who's gonna watch your back?"

"Don't underestimate Auntie Betty," I say, and we both laugh. Then Patrick gets serious.

"What do you need?" he asks.

"Watch out for my mother," I say. "Things have

gotten . . . pretty bad. Can you stop by every now and then and make sure she's okay? Huguette's going to be staying there, but just in case some heavy lifting needs to be done."

Patrick looks alarmed. "Why don't you take her to the doctor?"

"It's nothing a doctor can fix."

"How do you know if you've never taken her?"

We've had this conversation before and it's never ended well.

"It's too late for that," I say.

"Jesus, Quicksilver." Patrick shakes his head. "She's all you've got. Why the hell are you messing around?"

Patrick doesn't have a father either. We've never said it aloud, but both of us know: if something happens to one of our mothers, the other mother will take us in. It's an unspoken promise.

"Look, I'm going away so I can get her help. I can't explain, but I'm doing the complete opposite of messing around. Now stop asking me so many questions," I say.

Patrick swivels around on his stool and crosses his arms. He knows he's pushed me as far as he can.

"All right. So when are you coming back?" he asks.

"A month."

"You're going to miss the Heritage Festival," he says.

"Oh yeah, I forgot." I try to look like I care. But really, it's no loss for me. Everyone a couple. Every ride made for two. My quick escape when the festival closes and everyone searches for a dark and private place to hook up. Me in the parking lot trying to start my bike quietly so nobody will notice I'm leaving alone.

We finish our coffee in silence.

"So how's Meg?" I ask.

"She's good. She likes you a lot."

"She doesn't even know me."

"She knows you," says Patrick. "She knows me, so she knows you."

He's been telling me this for years, in restaurants or playgrounds, in the backseats of cars, on the beach and in the pool—that we are alike.

"You could bring her by," I say. "I could make tacos."

I indulge myself in a brief fantasy of this dinner, one that includes me with my new face. Maybe we're a four-some. Maybe I have a date too. I picture Meg laughing uproariously at something I've said. The fantasy quickly dissolves. It's a nice daydream, but it will never happen.

Being an outsider comes with gifts. The first is a special kind of vision that has nothing to do with being the son of Seers. I can see around the edges of things. Patrick, Meg, Susie Egan—their birthright is their future. Everything lies ahead of them, and they don't doubt for one moment that it's their due. They walk into the future without even knowing it's a privilege.

Me, I have no birthright here. Soon I will be left behind.

FOURTEEN

THE RECRUITER, LYSANDROS CARO, BETTER known as Sandros, is a large man in his fifties. Not fat, but big: barrel chest, round face, belt slung under his belly. First-generation Greek, he claims. Often he roams the corridors of the VRC, speaking in a thick accent, quoting his beloved grandmother Daphne. One of the old woman's favorites is, *When a part of you falls asleep, wake it up, for Christ's sake.* He makes bread with olive oil and brings in waxed bags of sweet buns from the Middle Eastern bakery. I always found his jocularity annoying, and it's even worse now that I know he's a big fat fake. He's Isaurian— no more Greek than me.

"So, young man," he says, on my coming into his office. "You've finally made it here. What took you so long?"

Then he abruptly sits forward, his chair squeaking, and riffles through my file as if searching for something, some small piece of paper that would tell him why he hasn't seen me until now. It's an act. He's waiting for me to fill the silence. Meanwhile I'm getting into character. I'm fully prepared to have a discussion about what methods of suicide I've been considering. Unfortunately, Sandros doesn't seem to have any interest in the particulars of doing oneself in.

He picks a leaf of basil and offers it to me. When I don't accept it, he tears the leaf into tiny bits and chews it into a bright green cud. He pours himself some hot water, squeezes some lemon into it, and takes meaningful sips. Finally, when it appears I have wasted both his time and my own, he says, "What it must be like for you, Thomas, living in this world with a face like that."

His voice is incredibly gentle and his words sum up my entire existence. Is this a question? A statement? An invitation? Whatever it is that he said, it creeps inside and begins loosening everything up. I never realized how buttoned up every little piece of me had to be in order to make it through each day. I begin to weep and once I start, I can't stop.

Do we say anything else? Do we discuss anything after that? I can't remember.

"Our time is up," says Sandros.

I look at the office clock: two hours have gone by. He scribbles something on a prescription pad.

Oh God, I've failed. He wants to medicate me. With trembling hands I read the script. *You must go to a world where you can be whole.*

There comes a point in time when all history and faces are one. Sitting in his office, I could have been all of the forgotten and given-up-on boys: boy who climbs in the wrong car and is never seen again, boy in juvenile hall pretending he's not afraid so he won't be stabbed with a plastic butter knife, boy who goes to war and never returns home. But no longer. Somebody has come to drag this boy into the light.

"I have a proposition for you," says Sandros. "Are you interested?"

"Yes," I answer.

"Then listen carefully," he says.

· PART ·
TWO

FIFTEEN

THE ROOM IS DISAPPOINTINGLY SMALL, the furnishings minimal. There are a chair, a table, a lamp, a green rug, and a tiny window through which a faint breeze blows. I focus on that window. I feel ensnared. Two days have passed since I've received the invitation to go to Isaura. Now the time has come to go, and the urge not to is over-whelming.

"Sit," says Sandros, gesturing to the chair.

What are we doing here? I expected the portal to be somewhere outside.

"I thought it would be different," I say. Sandros crosses his arms and frowns.

"You're one of the lucky ones. You can walk; you can breathe on your own. Most of the people I recruit are in wheelchairs. You expected the journey to be some kind of a wild, psychedelic ride?" he asks in his heavily accented English.

I nod, not trusting myself to answer. Even though I know he's not a Seer, I'm still afraid that any minute he will be alerted to the fact that I'm not who I appear to be.

"All right." Sandros lays a hand on my shoulder. "Time to go."

I can smell his cologne, some sort of musk. His hand

gets heavier on my shoulder. Soon it's weighing me down.

"Stop leaning on me," I struggle to say, trying to bat his bear paw of a hand away.

His scent becomes overpowering and I realize the legs of the chair are sinking into the carpet. With a grunt, Sandros pushes down on both of my shoulders hard.

"Go easy now," he says as I slide right through the floor with a pop.

It's every child's nightmare, getting trapped beneath the ice. But in my case I'm trapped beneath cheap maple flooring from Home Depot. Panicked, I scrabble with my hands at the flooring. I've changed my mind—I don't want to go. My heart thuds a fetal heartbeat. I feel like I've been buried alive.

I can see Sandros standing above me. "Please, no," I shout.

"You'll be fine," he mouths.

I won't be fine, but this realization comes too late. Within seconds an invisible undertow sucks me under and away. Sandros gets smaller and smaller as I travel into the matter that separates the worlds. I float down through shafts of amber light. The current imprints itself like a thousand hands on my body. Sometimes I manage to stay seated; other times I hang on to the wing-backed chair for dear life. For some reason, the chair has come with me on my journey—I have no idea why. Finally gravity prevails. I fall to the ground like some animal on all fours, my hands groping around for something solid to grasp.

"Quicksilver, Thomas," a voice says. "Welcome. You're the first to arrive."

SIXTEEN

I COLLAPSE ONTO MY STOMACH, EXHAUSTED.

"You have two minutes and forty-five seconds until the next immigrant is due," the voice adds. "Garabedian, Rose, arriving in a Pacesaver Scout electric wheelchair, model RF4. At the speed she's coming, her wheelchair could crush you. I suggest you move."

That gets me going. I spring to my feet and take a quick survey of my surroundings. I inhale feverishly, gulping in the smells like a deer, relying on a sort of animal GPS. My senses seem to have been amplified by passing through the portal and I'm assaulted by the forest landscape and its heady scents. Dizzy and disoriented, I stagger backward, fighting nausea.

What hits me first is the fundamental scent of Isaura,

a mixture of pine needles and sun. Somehow the smell is different from what it would be in America, more potent and energizing. Probably because there's no pollution in Isaura: it's the smell of a world that has remained stalwartly primitive. A part of me appreciates that, and a part of me despises it. I've grown rather attached to America, toxic waste and all.

"Once you're done retching, would you mind throwing your chair on the pile?" a voice asks.

I forgot I'm not alone. There's a large, muscular man standing next to a team of horses hitched up to a wagon. Another memory surfaces, threatening to topple me, and I see my father sitting in just such a wagon, leaning down to haul me up onto the seat beside him. I struggle to remain composed and move toward the man, my hand extended.

"No need for that," he says, averting his gaze. "Best way to help me out is to put your chair with the rest."

"I'm Thomas."

"I'm aware of that. You're on the list," he says.

"Who are you?" I ask.

"I'm Nigel 581. Please do as I ask."

It seems like business as usual. If the Isaurians are expecting me, they haven't let on yet.

Nigel points to a huge pile of items: wheelchairs,

walkers, slings, and canes—all the accoutrements of lives left behind. I lug the wing-backed chair over, where it looks ludicrously out of place.

Garabedian, Rose, arrives a minute later. She's a middle-aged woman wearing a flowered housedress.

"I'm here!" she cries, her eyes darting around wildly. I will later find out she has been paralyzed from the waist down since the age of twelve—clearly she had no qualms about leaving her life behind.

Nigel retrieves Rose, carries her to the cart, and props her up on pillows. He will carry her everywhere after she's Changed.

"Do I have to leave my wheelchair?" asks Rose.

I can imagine what she's feeling. The chair's her freedom. Plus it's probably expensive. I don't see how leaving it to rot in the woods will do anybody any good.

"Couldn't you use the parts for something?" I ask Nigel.

"What parts?"

"The motor?"

"We've got no need for motors," he says.

Unable to help myself, I snort with derision. I have little nostalgia for a world with no flush toilets, no screens to keep the mosquitoes out, no hot showers.

"You'll get used to it," says Nigel.

I won't be here long enough to get used to it, I want to

say. Instead I try and appear jaded. The truth is, I know more about this world than Nigel 581 ever will. I know all about the brutal control behind this pastoral simplicity.

I wonder how Isaura will appear to my fellow Changed. Will they notice the small differences that set the two places apart? The way the grass in Isaura is more blue than green? The way the sky has a lavender cast? The way the air seems thicker, stuffed with more molecules? All of this I have forgotten until now.

Four more immigrants arrive that day: Jerome and Jesse, co-joined twins who are fused at the chest; Michael, who weighs five hundred and eight pounds; and a girl named Emma, who has xeroderma pigmentosum, a hypersensitivity to ultraviolet light.

Once we're all settled in the wagon, Nigel clucks to the horses and we begin to move. A strange restlessness throbs inside me. It's like I've grown a second heart, one for each world I've lived in. I don't know if that's good or bad. Two hearts might come in handy if one of them fails. Then again, two hearts will mean twice the heartbreak.

I sit next to Emma, who has been allowed to keep the special clothing that protects her from the sun. She's younger, maybe eleven, and she's crying softly. All of us can hear her. I don't reach out to comfort her. None of us do. Right at that moment, we can think only of ourselves.

SEVENTEEN

"WHOA." NIGEL PULLS ON THE reins and the horses toss their heads. "The Laundry," he announces.

We've been traveling for over an hour. Nigel has stopped at a large wooden building with sliding doors. The smell of bleach permeates the air.

It's our first look at the Changed and my group stares at them in silence. I can tell they're taken aback at their beauty. They have a strange luminosity about them, as if the light around them is constantly being churned.

"Angels," whispers Emma.

"No," says Rose. "People just like us."

Although my group is enthralled with the Changed, we don't seem to inspire the same fascination. The Changed aren't looking at us; in fact, most of them are looking *beyond* us with careful gazes. Are they doing that in order to make us feel welcome? Often people do that with us freaks. They pretend they don't see our abnormalities. That's the worst. It's like pretending you don't see a skyscraper on fire. At the same time, you don't want someone screaming, "Call 911," when they see you. But the Changed used to *be* us. Don't they remember?

"Back to work," says Nigel, and the Changed obediently return to their giant cauldrons of steaming water.

The wagon rolls on. The countryside gleams as if it's been freshly scrubbed with Ajax and steel wool. Cardinals call to one another and locusts whir in the branches of the pine trees. There are meadows, furrowed potato fields, and manicured vegetable gardens. I can't help but be moved by Isaura's untouched beauty. That is, until I think about what this place did to my family.

I glance at Emma, who's curled up in a ball, no longer moving. Finally I shake off my self-absorption and place my hand on her back. She's so skinny I can see her shoulder blades right through her jacket. She shudders at my touch.

"We're almost there," I tell her. What can it be like never to have stood in the sun?

We drive by a lumberyard, a dairy, hay fields, and a barn. By the time the wagon arrives at the Compound, the rest of my group knows how they'll be spending their days: chopping wood and making soap, plowing and planting, weeding and harvesting, haying, threshing, and slopping pigs.

The wagon comes to a halt in front of a white clapboard building. The scent of baked apples comes wafting out. I can just visualize the cinnamon and the cream and the little pats of butter on top. My stomach begins to rumble and I want nothing more than to go inside and eat. Suddenly I feel terrified. I pinch the inside of my wrist hard enough to draw blood. I could sink down into that smell and lose myself. Forget why I have come. Baked apples are not for you, I remind myself. Finding your mother's Seerskin and getting the hell out is.

"Quicksilver, Thomas, climb down," instructs Nigel. "Your Host is here."

I clamber out of the wagon and stand in the dusty street, unsure of what to do next. A man materializes in the doorway of the building. He crooks his finger, beckoning me. "I'm Dash 482," the man says, sizing me up. "Let's go."

I hesitate.

"Now," he says menacingly, stepping out of the doorway.

It's too late to turn back. I obey.

EIGHTEEN

THE SIX OF US EAT alone that first night, like children getting their meal out of the way before the adults sit down with their wine and lamb chops. The Changed are still out on work detail; they won't return for another hour.

It can't be later than four in the afternoon and the sun streaming through the windows of the refectory is a soft pinkish gold. The light nudges me outside myself; I can't believe I'm back in Isaura. None of us speak. There's only the sound of silverware clinking against the pewter plates.

"Listen closely," says Dash, clapping to get our attention. "These are your Hosts." He gestures to the five men and women sitting with him at a circular table.

"You'll live with us during your first hundred days in Isaura. After that time you'll be assigned to dormitories. Let me warn you. There will be an adjustment. You may not find this easy. This is not America. None of us is rare here. None of us is exceptional or special. The sooner you realize this, the quicker your conversion will be. Do you understand?"

We nod like good Recruits.

"The longer you're here, the easier things will get. I can promise you that," says Dash. At that point, I tune out. I wriggle around impatiently in my chair. Dash doesn't notice; he's too busy proselytizing.

About ten minutes later he finally wraps up his little sermon.

"Look around you, then. This is your surrogate family. I suggest you get to know one another. It will be easier if you figure out what you have in common rather than what separates you," he says.

Dash pauses, trying to gauge whether he's getting through to us. His gaze falls on me. I attempt to look both worried and excited. He scowls. I'm not fooling him. Or maybe he can't see past my scar tissue.

"All groups meet once a week. Elect a foreman. Someone to represent you all." Dash waves his hand at us dismissively and sits down.

I size him up between bites of mashed potato. Dash is in his early twenties, lean but really fit, probably from chopping all that wood.

I remember the Host my mother and I saw that day we went to the Compound. The way he watched us, as if he were trying to memorize our faces. Perhaps he turned my parents in, somehow figured out that they were malcontents and tipped off the Ministry.

Other than Dash, the Hosts don't look like watchdogs at the moment, though. They look more like a group of Pennsylvania Dutch, getting ready to attend a barn raising. All of them wear brown canvas work pants and blue shirts. I feel rather than see their eyes descend on me. I turn my attention back toward the table.

Then Dash stands up again. "Forgot to mention," he drawls. "Tomorrow morning Nigel 581 will take you all to the Ministry. That's when you'll be Changed."

I drop my fork as a jolt of pure adrenaline races through my system, desperate to find some way out. Tomorrow? Somehow I never imagined the Change would happen right away.

Michael belches. His greasy hands hang from his wrists like two platters. "Pass the potatoes," he says.

Rose, the paralyzed woman, studies me. "Are you having second thoughts?" she asks me softly.

"Aren't you?" I say.

"I'm not," says Jesse.

"Me either," echoes Jerome loudly. "We can't wait to get the hell away from each other."

Suddenly Dash is standing at our table. "Who's having second thoughts?" he demands.

Like children keeping a secret from the teacher, none of us answer.

"You?" Dash asks me.

I shake my head. My heart is hammering.

"Well, I'm not sure I believe you, T. Everybody has second thoughts."

He called me "T." I haven't heard that name for nine years. Not since the day my father died. But how could Dash know about that? How could anyone know?

Dash waits for my response. I don't know what to say. Suddenly I don't feel capable of doing this. Masquerading as a Changed. Finding my mother's Seerskin. The walls of the room collapse and grow smaller.

"Um," I say.

"Eat, asshole," Jesse whispers.

I have the sudden urge to laugh hysterically. Instead I cram my mouth full of food.

We're all a little scared when the time comes to split up after dinner. We have known each other for only a few hours, but the intensity of our situation has united us.

Have you ever seen a five-hundred-pound man walk? It's a nearly impossible feat. Michael is able to take two or three steps and then he has to rest. He looks like he's about to suffocate—the effect of gravity on pendulous flaps of flesh. I try to help. I nearly fall under the weight of him until Jesse and Jerome prop up his other side.

"Thanks," I whisper.

"Nice teamwork," comments Dash, his hand under his chin, as if he's watching sperm swim around in a petri dish. Slowly we make our way to Nancy 499's house, where Michael's staying.

How can I best describe the Compound? Have you ever been to Sturbridge Village? Just like that, minus the gift shop where you can buy bayberry-scented room spray and horehound candy. The Compound is dotted with small clapboard buildings that are grouped around a central village green. Suddenly the air fills with voices. We stop in mid-stride, a parade of freaks, and the Changed are all around us.

"Let them pass," says Nancy.

They move around us like a current, intent on one thing: the Refectory. It's only then that I become aware of the gonging—the bell that signals the end of the workday. In a few minutes time the Refectory doors swing shut and the green is deserted again except for us.

All the Hosts have houses of their own; the rest of the Changed live in dormitories. Among the Changed the Hosts hold the power.

Dash and I are the last to go home. Finally I stand in his kitchen, my knees wobbling with exhaustion.

"Bathroom's outside. We've got running water. No electricity. You'll stay here."

He opens a door. My room contains a bed and a chair, little else. On the bed are two neatly folded piles of clothes and on the floor a pair of boots. There's one window that looks out on the green. There are no curtains. I'll have no privacy.

"You'll find two changes of clothes. They'll need to last you all week. Laundry is done on Saturdays," says Dash. He stands in the doorway, waiting. I squirm under his gaze. Am I supposed to do something? Give him a tip?

"Come on," he says, thrusting out his hand. "Get changed and give me your old clothes."

Oh no! My Barker's. I've smuggled it in. It's a tiny book, the size of my hand, and at the moment it resides in the back pocket of my jeans.

"Okay, just give me a minute," I say, moving to shut the door. I have to find somewhere to hide the primer.

"No," he says, stepping into the room. "In front of me."

"I've got to go to the bathroom." It's the only thing I can think of to say.

He snorts. "Get undressed."

"No, I mean it. If you don't let me go, I'll have an accident." I squeeze my legs together for emphasis.

"Jesus," he says, and moves aside.

I run to the outhouse. I look up and see he's watching

me from the window. I swing the wooden door shut behind me.

"Leave it open," he yells.

Luckily it's dark in the outhouse. I slide the Barker's out of my back pocket with one hand and undo my jeans with the other. There's only one place to hide the book. I bury it in the pail of lime. I'll have to retrieve it tomorrow.

"Move it, kid," Dash hollers.

When I get back to the room, I hurriedly strip down to my underwear and then I reach for the brown pants.

He holds out a burlap bag.

"Put your clothes in here."

I watch him eye my Levi's hungrily as I fold them into a square. He's probably sick to death of wearing those puffy pants. Here's my opportunity to make nice.

"They're yours," I say, handing them to him.

He takes my jeans and caresses the faded worn fabric with the fingers of his right hand. "Well, I'll be damned," he says. Then, with his left hand, he pulls me toward him and forcefully grabs the back of my neck.

"You think I want your cast-off jeans?" He grins. His teeth are perfect—thirty-two squares of peppermint gum.

"No, sir. I just thought you might be tired—"

Dash drops the jeans to the floor. "What kind of a game are you playing, T?"

"No game," I say, trying to wriggle out of his grasp.

"I don't believe you, kid. How're you going make me believe?" He leans forward, his breath a hot vapor in my face.

Panic makes my skin tingle. Things have escalated again suddenly. "Look, I was just trying to be nice," I say.

"For Christ's sake," says Dash. He stares at my face and his nose wrinkles with repulsion. "How long ago did that happen?"

"When I was a kid," I say.

"Bet you don't have many friends."

"No. No, I don't," I say.

"Ever kissed a girl?"

"I don't see how that's relevant," I say in a soft, tremulous voice. Then I screw up my face as best as I can (which is not easy to do when your skin is all puckered), as if I'm close to tears. For the record, I'm not; I've withstood far worse lines of questioning.

Dash gives me a disgusted look, then releases me so quickly I topple to the floor.

"You, my friend, better get with the program," he says. "Know what the program is?"

I nod. My eyes are watering nicely. Dash is all blurry.

"Oh, stop your bawling," barks Dash.

I fold my jeans and T-shirt into a neat pile, stuff them in the burlap sack, and hand it back to him.

After Dash leaves my room and the sound of his footsteps recede, I let the upper half of my body fall back on the bed. My feet I keep firmly planted on the floor. I've made it to Isaura and past my Host, at least for now.

NINETEEN

"Showtime," says Dash.

I wake to find him standing over me in the dark.

I sit up, totally disoriented. I've only been in Isaura for six hours, yet it feels like a week. I have been dreaming about Patrick teaching me a wrestling move called the Tombstone Pile Driver. I want to stay in the dream. It seemed so real I could smell the school gym: the rubber, sweat, and Dorito stench.

All the Hosts and my fellow immigrants are waiting for us outside. Because it's night I see Emma for the first time. She's taken off her gloves and pulled back her hood. The ends of her long curly brown hair are wet from where she's sucked on them. She smiles at me shyly.

The green has undergone a transformation as I've slept. A stage has been erected. Torches now line the cobblestone walkways and the entire population of the Compound has been assembled. By the looks of it, they're waiting for us.

Michael's Host, Nancy, sticks him with her elbow. "You first."

Michael lets out a soft groan.

"I don't think I can do it," he whispers. His forehead beads up with sweat. He breathes heavily, nervously looking across the green at the crowd.

"Sure, you can," Jerome says. "Hundred feet, that's all. Hundred steps, it'll be over. Come on, we'll count them together."

Emma takes Michael's hand. He pats her head like she's a small animal.

There are two long rows of benches and a center aisle set up in front of the stage. We have to walk down that center aisle to make it to the bench designated for us. Those last twenty feet are interminable. I can't help but feel this is a church and we are the motley wedding party. Luckily we lurch forward without having to endure any gawking. The Changed barely move. They sit gazing intently forward as if watching some movie only they can see. There are two empty benches up front. We sit in the front row and our Hosts sit behind us.

Dash leans forward and taps me on the shoulder. "Tonight you'll be witnessing," he whispers. "We do this once a month."

I get a sick feeling in my stomach. Witnessing. It has a religious ring to it.

"Welcome," squeaks a voice. The curtains slide open to reveal an ancient man sitting on a tattered and stained red velvet chair. There's only a smattering of applause, as if the real star has been delayed and this act will now have to be endured.

"For those of you who have just arrived, I am Geld 32,783," he says. Then he shakes his head. "No, Geld 32,784." He looks upward as if consulting someone. "I think that's right," he mutters.

I do a quick calculation in my head. This man has been in Isaura for almost ninety years!

The Changed begin whispering and soon they are having outright conversations. Geld doesn't seem to notice. He keeps speaking, but his voice gets softer and softer, and soon I can't hear anything he's saying. I have the urge to steamroll right over him too. I turn to Emma and ask, "Did you enjoy dinner?"

I can't believe I'm asking her something so stupid.

"Yes, I did," she says brightly.

"Did you prefer the green beans or the corn?" I continue.

"Oh, corn!" she declares, looking like she's about to break into song and tap-dance.

I keep glancing back at Geld, who seems to shrink in size the longer he sits up there and the louder the audience gets. Finally he's taken away. Once he's out of sight, everyone becomes quiet again and I feel ashamed for ignoring him.

"My name is Mitsuko," says a voice from behind me.

I swivel around in my seat and see a tall Japanese woman striding up the aisle. Her long hair is wound up in two buns on her head. She wears the regulation brown pants and blue shirt, but she doesn't wear the boots; she's barefoot.

"I've been Changed for ninety-nine days," she says, walking onto the stage. She looks in our direction but doesn't actually see us. It's more of a sweeping glance that makes it appear as if she does.

"Honored Hosts." She bows deeply.

Nancy 499 stands.

"I am ready for the questions," says Mitsuko.

"Why don't you go back to the place you came from?" asks Nancy. "You have free choice. You can leave anytime."

"I don't leave because I can do this!" Mitsuko cries. She lifts her arms over her head, does three quick handsprings, and lands in a split.

A jolt of pleasure courses through me. When I see someone do something extraordinary, it makes me want to do something extraordinary too. The Changed do not share my pleasure. Murmurings of disapproval reverberate through the crowd.

"Mitsuko 99, I would expect this kind of behavior from a 24, not somebody who's nearing the hundred-day mark. The three Rs," Nancy says.

Mitsuko collects herself. She presses her palms together as if in prayer.

"Ruined by chance, Redeemed by invitation, Regenerated by work," she recites, her head submissively bowed.

Nancy nods her approval as if she were Chairman Mao.

The testimonials go on all evening and each one ends with a recitation of the three Rs. The last two Rs are always the same, but the first can be answered either "Ruined by chance" or "Ruined by genetics." I guess in this way they account for both tragic accident and cellular abnormality. Finally it's over and everyone begins filing out of the benches and making their way to the dormitories except for us. Dash tells us to wait. He disappears for a moment and comes back with a bearded man.

"This is Adam 856," says Dash. "He's been sketching you."

"Your name?" Adam asks Rose. He's carrying a pad of paper.

"Rose Garabedian?" she says like a question.

"That's the last time you'll answer that way," says Dash. "Tomorrow you'll be Rose 1."

Adam writes Rose's name on the pad. Then he tears off the piece of paper and places it in her lap. Rose's chin wobbles as she looks at the sketch of herself, her legs strapped to a wooden chair.

"Why are you doing this?" I ask. "She doesn't need a reminder of how she looks. That's why she came here."

Tears stream down Rose's face.

"It's my job," Adam says. "What's your name?"

I shake my head. I don't want my sketch.

"Everyone has it done," says Dash. "There has to be a record."

"Your name," repeats Adam.

I refuse to answer.

"Thomas Quicksilver," Dash answers for me.

Adam scrawls my name on the pad, tears off the page, and hands it to me. I hand it back.

"You got it wrong. That's not my name. My name's Pucker," I say.

Dash scowls but says nothing.

TWENTY

AND THEN I SEE HER. She's standing in the aisle, her head tilted to one side as if she's waiting for a cab.

I've never seen a girl with a gaze like this. It streams from her eyes creek-cold and clear as a November night. She has the look of someone who could have lived in the nineteenth century—no, all the centuries that have ever passed. She's long necked and has a generous mouth. Hundreds of lunar moths hover above her in the trees. Even though she's standing still, she appears to be moving.

My cells feel like they're being rearranged and I can only think of one thing: I can't let this girl see me before I get my new face.

"Hurry up," I say, trying to move Michael along, hoping she hasn't seen me yet.

There's no rushing a five-hundred-pound man and it's too late anyway: the girl is staring at us openly. She's the first Changed (other than our Hosts) to have done so. In the minutes it takes us to reach her, my heart beats out a tattoo of distress. I think of my favorite painters. I recite them like a litany: Caravaggio, Magritte, Vermeer, and Modigliani. The musicality of their names calms me.

"Hello there," I say as we approach, and immediately cringe. I sound like a librarian.

She sticks out her hand. I go to shake it and she quickly withdraws her arm, leaving me hanging. Had we known each other, had we been old friends this would have been funny. But given our circumstances, it's hostile.

"That wasn't very nice, Phaidra. Keep it up and you'll have to go through orientation again," says Dash.

Phaidra looks at Dash with amusement, her arms folded across her chest. Around her neck she wears a delicate filigree chain. I know from my *Barker's* that all the personal possessions of immigrants are confiscated. I wonder how and why she got away with keeping it.

"It's all right," I say, not wanting her to get into trouble.

Dash turns to Phaidra. "Shouldn't you be getting back to the dorm?"

She shrugs.

"Let me rephrase that. Get back to the dorm," he says.

Phaidra shrugs again, as if nothing he could ever say would matter, then saunters off slowly.

Dash watches her go, and, despite myself, I watch her as well.

"She's trouble. Get her out of your mind right now," says Dash.

"She wasn't in my mind."

"Sure, she wasn't."

Phaidra is so beautiful it's hard to imagine she was ever not that way. "Why's she here?" I ask.

"You mean what was wrong with her?" says Dash. He smirks. "I'll never tell. That's rule number one. We don't discuss what brought us here. That's why none of the Changed looked at you tonight. You're invisible until you're Changed."

"Then why wasn't I invisible to Phaidra?"

Dash rummages around in his pockets. "No idea. Must be something special about you. That what you want to hear? She saw beneath your monstrous face to your handsome, noble self?" He pulls out a pack of cigarettes, shakes one out, and places it between his lips.

That's *exactly* what I had hoped.

"You were Phaidra's Host?" I guess.

Dash peers at me through squinted eyes and inhales deeply. "Aren't you the perceptive one?"

"You had her before me?"

I cringe when I say this, realizing how it sounds. What I meant to ask was if Phaidra had been Dash's recruit before me.

Dash knows exactly what I meant, but he decides to toy with me. He laughs cryptically. "You could say that."

Jealousy rockets through me. I can taste it in my mouth, dirty and copperish. This is crazy. I've just met the girl, but I can't stand the thought that Dash has been with her. Now the necklace makes sense. She has it because he let her keep it.

"She's had a hard time giving up her wild ways. If she doesn't watch herself, she's going be in a boatload of trouble," says Dash.

I wonder what a "boatload of trouble" means here among the Changed. How is punishment meted out? I don't know. But one thing I do know is that the brighter the shine, the bigger the shadow—and Phaidra glows like a klieg light.

TWENTY-ONE

I SNEAK OUT THAT NIGHT to do reconnaissance. Partly because I need to find out if I *can* sneak out and partly because I'm going stir-crazy. By eight that evening Dash is snoring away.

I'd forgotten about this. Everyone goes to sleep early in Isaura because once it gets dark, there's nothing to do. I have little desire to sit around the kitchen table and watch the candle burn down to a stub. Dash has locked me in my room, which I find more than a little creepy, but I climb out the window easily enough and drop to the ground.

Tonight I intend to find my way back to the portal. I want to make sure that it's still there and that I can get back on my own.

I get lost, but eventually I find the tunnel. It's deserted, completely unguarded. I guess no one ever tries to sneak out of Isaura; I find this really depressing. I walk through the tunnel and stick my hand out into the cone of shimmering light that pours down from the sky. The air nips at me gently, like a kitten.

It's a perfect summer night. I'm seventeen years old. I should have no cares other than what I'm going to do on Saturday night. But that is not my life. That has never been my life.

I step into the light. I think of our apartment. Its worn couches, its blender and coffeemaker. The electricity, the invisible current of energy that warms us and keeps our rooms lit. The portal begins to tug on me. I stagger backward and grab the hedgerow with two hands. I can't stop thinking of my mother. What's happening to her now? Are the visions coming so quickly and in such a torrent that she's no longer even conscious?

"Take care of her, Huguette," I whisper as I thrust myself back into the tunnel. It's like climbing down into a manhole, dank and musty, and I'm flooded with despair.

I run back to Dash's house. I shouldn't have wasted this night. I should have gone straight to the Ministry to begin my search for my mother's skin. Why didn't I do that? It's that girl's fault. That beautiful girl with the strange name.

I want—I *want* so many things.

TWENTY-TWO

W HEN I WAKE, I REMEMBER that this is the day I'll be Changed. The first thing I do is vomit because I'm so nervous.

During the years after the fire I took comfort in imagining that I wasn't alone—that there was a whole tribe of people like me who were whole before they were not. Who were these others? I romanticized them. A painter who knew the precise shade of alizarin crimson before he went blind, a violinist who mastered Paganini's 24 Caprices before she went deaf. We were a different species than those who were born disfigured because we remembered a time when it wasn't so. Whether the ability to remember would eventually drive us mad, I didn't know.

Suddenly I remember my Barker's, which I hid in the outhouse. I ask permission to go to the bathroom and Dash looks at me like I'm crazy. Now that it's daylight, he doesn't seem to be keeping such a close eye on me.

I'm relieved to find the book is still buried in the bucket of lime. After a few minutes of deliberation (and after realizing that my new Isaurian pants have no pockets), I decide it's best to leave it there. When I come into the kitchen, Dash hands me a cup of hot tea. It's a small house; obviously he heard me throwing up. We eat our breakfast in silence.

It's raining when Nigel pulls up to the house. I go to the window; the wagon's been covered with a mottled gray canvas.

"I'll be here when you return," says Dash, placing his mug in the sink.

I nod. I feel sick again.

"It doesn't hurt," he says.

"Whatever." I don't believe him.

"I'm telling you the truth."

"Okay, okay." Now he's irritating me. I just want to go and get it over with.

I'm the last to be picked up. Nobody says a word as I climb aboard the wagon. Once we get going again, Emma scoots next to me. She presses a photograph into my hand: it's of her parents sitting in a rowboat. Of course, Emma is nowhere in sight, because the photo was taken in the daytime. She must have been in the lodge. Or perhaps they went on vacation without her, left her in a house with tinted windows that filtered out ultraviolet light. The photograph sickens me. I'm in a terrible mood this morning.

"You shouldn't have brought this. They'll take it away if they find it," I tell her.

She ignores me. "That's Jewel Lake. My father told me there were jewels at the bottom of it. He brought me back one." She smirks. "He said he dove down to the bottom and found it. A blue topaz, my birthstone. He made it into a ring. But I couldn't bring it with me. The Recruiter said no jewelry."

I don't know what to say to her. All I want is to tune out.

Emma takes the picture back, holds it up to her face, and examines it. "There, see?" she says.

I sigh. "See what?"

"That space, between my parents. That's for me."

"I don't see any space." Her parents are crammed up against each other, their shoulders and thighs touching, bathing in the sunlight while their daughter is sitting alone in the dark.

"No, there's a space," she says, her voice breaking. "Mama told me so. They left room for me."

She begins to cry.

Rose looks over at me and scowls. *Do something,* she mouths. I shrug. I don't want to get involved. But Emma's weeping gets annoyingly loud.

"Lemme see." I take the picture and pretend to study it. "Oh yeah, now I see."

"You do not!" Emma shouts, grabbing it back. "You lie and you suck!"

"Give it here," says Michael. He takes the picture and shows it to Rose.

"Oh yes, dear. I see. They've made a space for you, all right. There on the cushion, under the warm sun," Rose murmurs.

"I'm sorry, Emma," I say after a few minutes.

She glares at me. "You must be really scared."

I look out of the back of the wagon. It's raining so hard it could be night. I see lanterns up ahead. A herd of cows suddenly materializes; then, just as quickly, they vanish into the fog.

"People get mean when they get scared," she says.

"I'm not scared," I say softly.

"Yes you are," she replies.

TWENTY-THREE

WHEN I GET MY FIRST glimpse of the Ministry— that enormous stone bulwark, far taller than any other building in the city—something inside me begins to throb. Suddenly breathing through my nose is not an option. I open my mouth like a dog and pant as quietly and unobtrusively as I can. Michael watches me guardedly, one arm slung protectively around Emma. I have failed to impress him this morning.

What I'm experiencing is nostalgia. It pierces through me, and while the initial thrust of memory is like a tiny knife stabbing into my side, something that has been dammed up is finally free.

I have forgotten nothing. Somewhere inside me I

have stored every detail. The wagon lumbers down the city streets and I know that to the left of me is the cobbler's shop and to the right of me is the blacksmith. The sounds of Isaura are a long-forgotten sound track that now crackles into life: the hollow whoosh of the bellows, the dull thud of a mallet hitting wood, the flapping of clothes strung up on a line.

My past is a giant who has been asleep for a thousand years. Now see his limbs twitch. Now see his stone face turn to flesh.

My smugness begins to melt away. Yes, I buy my shoes at the mall and we get our oil changed at Jiffy Lube and Isaura's insistence on hardship masquerading as purity annoys me. But as I continue to look out on the city streets, I can't help but remember all the good things: the community feasts, the long tables overflowing with food, sticking out my hand to get my future read, knowing that I was safe, that nothing would ever happen to me that I wouldn't be forewarned about.

The wagon jerks to a stop.

"Thomas?" says Rose.

I feel like an overcooked hot dog.

"Thomas," Rose repeats. "Nobody can leave until you do."

Nigel comes around the back of the wagon. "We don't have all day," he says.

I nod but don't move.

"Oh, for Christ's sake," says Michael, pushing me aside. "Get out."

Luckily for me, we don't have to travel far inside the Ministry. If we did, I think I might drown in my memories. Nigel leads us down the main corridor and tells us to sit down and wait. He raps twice on a closed door and a muffled voice says to bring Rose in first. He carries her in.

No more than twenty minutes pass before she's done. The door creaks open eerily. No sign of the Maker, but we see Rose, still sitting in her chair. She turns to look at us, smiles, and slowly stands. As she pulls herself upright, the years pour down her body and land in a puddle at her feet. I've made a mistake: she's young—younger than my mom.

Michael's called next. His Change takes longer. How many millions of calories did he consume over the years? How many Oreos, pancakes, and Cinnabons were in his past?

I tap my fingers nervously on my thigh as I wait. What if I don't fool the Maker?

When the new and improved svelte Michael comes out of the room, he sits down beside me, biting the inside of his cheek with joy. "Never again," he whispers triumphantly. "Those sons of bitches."

I know the ones he means: the same ones who christened me Pucker.

Emma's next. She's in the room for a far longer time, I assume because she was ruined by genetics, not tragedy. The change isn't obvious when she returns. She looks out the window, dismayed. It's still raining.

"I think it'll clear by this afternoon," Rose says.

Emma runs to Rose and buries her face in her lap. Startled but pleased, Rose strokes the girl's hair while gazing at her legs in wonder.

Jerome and Jesse are called next. I'm frustrated; their chests are fused together—their Change could take hours. And why am I last?

I can't sit still any longer. I get up and begin to pace. Lost in my thoughts, I don't notice the way my newly issued boots rat-a-tat-tat like gunfire on the wooden floor. Suddenly the door at the end of the hallway bursts open and a man well over six feet tall strides out, blue robes billowing around him.

As he stalks toward me I see how old he is, how lined his face is, and for a moment I'm relieved. Why, he's just a geezer, I think, but every step he comes closer, I'm made aware of the fact that old does not mean weak. Then I realize this is Otak. The High Seer of Isaura. The man who killed my father and flayed my mother of her skin. And—according to my Barker's—the man who sees all.

I immediately lose all sense of objectivity and cool. I'm afraid he'll recognize my burned face. I have to be Changed now! I run to the Maker's door and pound on it.

"Hurry," I cry.

The door doesn't budge. I lean my ear against the wood. I can't hear anything. What's taking so long?

"Thomas," whispers Rose. "Sit down. It'll be all right."

"It won't," I say. It's all over. The old man will take one look at me, remember Serena Gale's child who was burned, and I'll be discovered.

"Who is your Host?" asks Otak, towering over us. "Didn't they tell you how to conduct yourself in the Ministry?"

The Obedient Child is quiet at all times in the Ministry. How could I have forgotten?

He looks me over carefully. God, what if he touches me? What if he reads me? I know we're distantly related and it should be impossible, but what if he can do it anyway?

"He's scared," says Emma, looking Otak straight in the eye. "You shouldn't pick on people when they're scared."

This is bad: I need an eleven-year-old girl to defend me. I don't dare lift my head. I can feel his eyes boring into my skull.

"What's your name?"

"Tom Quicksilver," I tell him, thinking that if I do look familiar, the shortened version of my name might throw him off.

There's a long silence. Finally he speaks again.

"How were you burned?"

"There was a fire in my school," I lie.

"What, no fire alarms?" he asks.

"They forgot to change the batteries?" I offer up pathetically.

Otak raps on the Maker's door. "Finish up. There's one in agony out here. And you . . ." He turns back to face me. "Stop hiding."

I look up, terrified, but there's no glint of recognition. Only pity.

"Out of the darkness of unknowing and into the light of certainty," he says, raising his hand and punching it in the air.

He has hundreds of tiny stars sewn into his flesh.

TWENTY-FOUR

I'M SHOCKED TO FIND OUT the Maker is a teenage girl. When I lived in Isaura, the Maker was an old woman; that one must have died.

"Sit down," the Maker says.

She scoots her chair close to mine. She can't be more than fifteen. Like Otak, she has a Seerskin, but hers is copper hued. She notices me staring at her skin.

"You think it's strange," she says.

"Yes," I tell her.

"Our skins protect us. Without them we'd go mad," she explains.

"Really?" I say, trying to sound like I don't have first-hand experience with this.

"Yes, really," she says coolly. "You may call me Alice."

"Alice," I repeat. Already I feel her power. It's like I'm being hypnotized.

"I need you to close your eyes," she says.

She looks exhausted, probably from Changing all the others in my group. I imagine she just wants to get this last one over so she can go home.

I close my eyes and wait. Nothing happens. I squint like a pirate, taking a peek.

She's cradling her head in her hands. "I'm sorry," she says. "Give me a moment."

We sit in silence.

"Are you all right?" I ask after a while.

She looks up at me wearily. "You feel things?"

"Uh, yes," I say.

"Like love?"

"I guess. Well, sometimes," I add, wanting to paint a fair picture. "On holidays, mostly." This is sad but true.

She frowns, dissatisfied with my answer. "Affection?"

"Yes."

"Remorse? Regret?"

"Sure," I say slowly, not knowing where this is going.

She shakes her head, as if making some decision.

"Often I have wondered what it would be like to be governed by your emotions. I've felt sorry for your people that they are so imprisoned and grateful that it's not so for us."

"Okay," I say, aware she's on the cusp of revealing something. Should I try to say something funny? Attempt to cheer her up? But she isn't sad; she isn't capable of it. Perhaps she's trying to be and this is the point of the conversation.

Alice takes a few deep breaths and collects herself. "I'm sorry. Close your eyes again. This shouldn't take long." She reaches out for me and I wince involuntarily, terrified she will know who I am the moment she touches me. I hold up my hand.

"Give me a second," I say.

She gives me a strange look but nods. I close my eyes, trying willfully to empty myself of memory.

"Ready?" she asks finally.

"Yes," I say.

She presses her hands flat against my chest and her gift, as sleek and insistent as a pike, twists down inside me, probing. She's searching for the fire. I said I'd let her in, but now that the moment is approaching, I fight it with everything that I have. She's intent on tearing down the walls of my history; I'm intent on keeping them up.

"You've got to help," she whispers. "I don't know why, but I'm having trouble finding it. It should be here, but it's not."

"I can't," I cry. Suddenly I'm deathly afraid of sharing the fire and it's not for the reason I thought. It's because the fire is mine; it made me who I am—Pucker. What will I do without the defining event of my life?

"You must," she says firmly. "Give me one detail. A smell. A color. That's all I need to find my way in."

I shudder. It's exactly as my mother told me. I give her the curtains. The burned-nut smell of the fabric going up in flames.

"Here we go," she says.

My head feels like it's swarming with butterflies.

"I'm going to give you something to distract you while I work," says the Maker. "It's not reality. It never really happened to you. People from Earth tell me it's like watching a movie," she explains, her voice getting fainter.

I fall back, into her manufactured memory.

I'm lying in bed. I'm four years old. I have to pee, really, really bad. It's the middle of the night. The room is dark. I'm too scared to get up and go to the bathroom. I hold my urine and pray for morning. I think of things opposite of water— hard things like books, granite, lollipops, and ice. But finally the pee comes in a torrent. The pleasure of surrender. Warmth. Then terror. I will be punished. I hide under the blankets, trying to muffle the sounds of my sobbing. I hear the sound of my mother's footsteps. I go rigid and lie perfectly still. Maybe she'll forget I'm here. Maybe she won't smell the piss.

No such luck. She pulls down my covers and I'm exposed. I whimper in fear. She doesn't spank me; instead she gathers me up into her arms and says she loves me, I'm her boy, nothing I do could make her

angry. My Bonnie lies over the ocean. My Bonnie
lies over the sea. . . .

I hear the Maker gasp.

My face. Something is happening to my face.

"Don't open your eyes. We're not done yet," she warns.

Molten orange and red. Bayberry candles.

"Hold still. Hold very still."

Just one. One more strip of skin. Brace your-
self; I'll pull quickly and it will be over.

Darkness so dense I think I will suffocate.

Breathe, says my nurse Clara Graves. Just breathe.

My boy.

Wreathed in flames.

My beautiful boy.

"Done," says Alice.

TWENTY-FIVE

The Maker holds up a mirror. At first I can see only one feature at a time: a cheekbone, an eyebrow, a nose, my temple. Each feature on its own is unremarkable, but put all of them together and the effect is startling. I'm a study in autumnal colors: longish brown hair, green eyes, black lashes, olive skin. Framed in light, I am stunning. I'm not being arrogant—this is the truth.

I wonder if Alice gave me more than I was due. A little something extra to make up for all the years of good face I have missed.

"It's all you," says Alice, though I haven't spoken. "I didn't give you anything that wasn't yours." But even she looks flabbergasted at the result. When I come out of the room, I hang my head. Not in shame, but in embarrassment. I've received too much.

"Look at me," says Rose gently.

I can tell by the tone of her voice that she thinks the Maker has failed. Slowly I raise my head and she gasps and I have my first experience of being seen. The sensation is like being inhaled. I have to hold very still in order to come back to myself.

"Why, Thomas," she says. "You're a knockout."

"Stud," says Jesse, whacking me on the shoulder. He's grinning wildly and I can see he's kidding. He doesn't care what I look like as long as he isn't fused to his brother any longer.

When we climb back into the wagon, the rain's stopped. Steam rises off the cobblestones and blue patches of sky scuttle above us. Nigel stares at us openly;

I guess we're worthy of his attention now. I don't pay much attention to Isaura on the way back to the Compound; I'm too preoccupied with my new face. I keep touching it. The skin on my cheeks is so soft. I wonder if I'll have to shave.

It's early evening by the time we return to the Compound. One by one we're dropped off at our houses. True to his word, Dash is waiting in the kitchen.

"I knew it," he says.

"Knew what?" I ask cautiously.

"That you'd come back looking like that. The uglier you are when you go in, the bigger the Change. They made you a bit too pretty, I'm afraid." He circles me. "Girls don't like it if you're better looking than them."

"I didn't come here for the girls," I mutter.

"Sure, you didn't, kid."

Dash yanks a sweater over his head. "Dishes need to be done and the wood bin needs filling. You got a problem with that, Thomas 1?"

"Did I do something to make you mad?" I ask.

"Jesus, stop being such a baby. Just clean up," he says. Then he goes out on the front porch and lights up.

I finish my chores and wait for Dash to come back in so I can sneak out. But he never does. He smokes cigarette after cigarette and two hours later I drift off to sleep, my arm flung over my new face protectively, as if I'm afraid of someone stealing it in the middle of the night.

TWENTY-SIX

THE NEXT MORNING I STAND in the entrance of the Refectory wondering where I should sit.

"Thomas," yells Jesse, waving me over.

I can feel everybody looking at me as I make my way down the aisle. I keep my hands down at my sides, not wanting anybody to see the big wet patches under my arms. I'm nervous and incredibly self-conscious and there's no such thing as deodorant in this backward world. The rest of my group is already assembled. Dash sits at a table with the other Hosts. He gives me a jaunty salute as if to say, *Glad you could make it.*

"Where've you been?" asks Michael as I sit down. Clearly my tardiness annoys him.

"I overslept," I say, shooting Dash a dirty look.

I'd slept fitfully that night, not knowing what was real and what was dream. I guess Dash saw no need to make sure I got to the Refectory on time.

I'm starving. Everyone's already eaten. An empty platter sits in the middle of the table. I look around, hoping to signal somebody to refill it, but the kitchen is closed.

"Here." Jerome stabs a piece of his sausage with his fork and plunks it on my plate.

"Where's the coffee?" I ask.

"Over there." Rose points to Dash's table.

"You're kidding me," I say as it becomes clear only the Hosts are allowed coffee. I groan. This is a disaster.

"Um, excuse me, hello," says a voice, interrupting my thoughts.

I look up into the brown eyes of a teenage girl.

"I'm Tammi 622," she says.

She's pretty. Long blond hair, a smattering of freckles, ears that stick out the tiniest little bit. She hands me a square card imprinted with the number 7 on it.

"Will you accept?" she asks.

"Accept what?"

Jesse leans across the table. "Are you crazy? Who cares what she wants? Just say yes."

"Okay," I say. "Yes." I hand the card back to her.

"No. You keep it," she says. "You have to give it to your Host."

Tammi is pushed aside by a petite girl with short

black hair and a tattoo of a grapevine that creeps across her neck like a garden snake. "I'm Lina 231. Will you accept?"

I don't know what's going on, but it's clear I'm in demand: for what I'm not sure. I glance up and see Phaidra sitting a few tables away. Nobody sits on either side of her and I can tell why: she's radiating get-the-crap-away-from-me vibes. She peers down at her empty plate with feigned interest.

I turn back to Lina.

"Well?" she asks.

Her card reads *7:30*. So, the number signifies a time.

"What's happening at seven thirty?"

Lina gives me a funny look. "Are you open to receiving callers or not?"

Callers? These girls are asking me for dates! I glance at Phaidra again—now I'm sure she's purposely ignoring what's going on at my table.

"Sure. Why not," I say loudly, placing her card on top of Tammi's.

As soon as I say this, I'm plagued with guilt. I'm here to find my mother's Seerskin; I've got no business arranging dates. I reassure myself with the thought that I've got to play along, convince them all that I'm here for good.

By the time breakfast is over, I've collected a tidy stack of cards. Now I seek shelter in my plate like Phaidra, but I cast my eyes downward in embarrassment.

My group's silent. They don't have to speak for me to know what they are thinking. What do you say to someone who's winning at blackjack while you're stuck beside them playing the penny slots?

Dash comes over to our table. "Well, you've caused quite a stir with the ladies, young Thomas."

There he goes again, acting like he's my grandfather. I half expect him to start calling me "lad."

He thrusts out his hand for the cards. "I'll take those."

I hand them over.

He riffles through them quickly. "Looks like somebody will be busy this week. Gotta get you some protection, boy," he says loudly, his voice slicing through the din in the Refectory. He claps me on the back like we're frat mates. Mortified, I shrink away from him. Protection? Is he talking about a chaperone? A guard?

"Rule number five, what is it?" he shouts.

Nobody answers.

"Come on, people!"

Still no answer. Dash sounds exactly like my history teacher, Mr. Laird. In that moment I wish fervently that I were sitting in that class being ignored.

Phaidra springs to her feet. "Rule number five, section eight, line two. Breeding is not allowed among the Changed."

Breeding? Wait a second. *Protection.* He's talking about birth control!

Dash looks amused and pleased. Obviously he hadn't expected Phaidra to supply the answer. "Correct. And why is that so?"

"The second R. We are Redeemed by invitation and invitation only. If you are born here, there is no opportunity for Redemption."

Dash smiles. Phaidra's making him look good in front of the rest of the Hosts.

"I see you took something from your hundred days with me," he says.

Phaidra nods obediently. "Certainly I did. Whether I shall turn out to be the hero of my own life, or whether that station will be held by anybody else, these pages must show," she says, and then sits down.

She's quoting Dickens, but Dash doesn't get it. He just assumes Phaidra is making fun of him (which she is).

"From *David Copperfield*," I whisper, trying to help him save face.

"Think I give two shits about some worthless magician?" he snaps.

I have to bite my lip to keep from laughing. "Worthless? I don't know about that. He did make the Statue of Liberty disappear," I say.

Dash's face fills with blood. What's wrong with me? I'm supposed to be flying under the radar, not doing cartwheels above it.

"I'm sorry. I'm not used to this kind of attention," I say quickly.

Dash glares at me, his jaw clenched. The other Hosts watch our encounter from across the room. One of them holds up Dash's coffee mug and waves him over. He leaves and Emma gives an audible sigh of relief.

"Guess you're not scared anymore," she says.

"Just stupid," comments Jerome.

"Why did you provoke him?" Michael asks angrily.

"I don't know," I say, realizing I've put my whole group at risk. If I keep it up, they might not send just me back, but the entire batch of us.

"I'm sorry. It won't happen again," I say.

Michael isn't satisfied with my apology. "You like quotes?" he asks. "You seem like a bookish kind of guy. Here's one. God dispenses beauty even to the wicked."

"God's got nothing to do with it," I say. He thinks I've gotten more than my due.

"Maybe, maybe not," Michael says as the gong begins to sound, signaling breakfast is over.

"No maybes about it. The Maker didn't pull my face out of thin air. This is how I would have looked if I hadn't been burned," I say.

Michael's newly exposed cheekbones flame scarlet. "And this isn't who I really am? That's what you're trying to say?"

I shrug. "Well, you weren't ruined by chance, were you?"

"No, I was ruined by genetics. My mother is obese and so was my grandmother," he says.

I shake my head. "No, you were ruined by a lack of willpower."

Michael flies to his feet and Rose grabs his arm and holds him back. She shakes her head. Slowly he sits down.

"You better watch your step," he says. "You need us."

"We need each other," says Rose.

TWENTY-SEVEN

WE WALK OUT TO THE GREEN. I'm shaken from my encounters with Dash and Michael, but I can't let it show.

It's only eight in the morning and I'm going to have to get through the entire day before I can go look for my mother's Seerskin. I know now that I've made a huge mistake. The first night I was here, I should have gone straight to the Ministry to find her skin and then gotten out of Isaura before I was Changed.

Things are a hundred times more complicated now. Now people want things from me. Even worse, I know what it is to have an external existence. Now *I* have skin, protection, something to shield me. The very thing my mother has sent me to find for her, I've found for myself.

Dash interrupts my reverie to tell me I'm to be a carpenter. I'm stunned. I don't know the first thing about woodworking. Trying to put off the inevitable, I ask Dash what made them choose me for this particular assignment since I'm so clearly unqualified.

"Jesus, are you self-involved," he says. "Look around you. Think any of these people were qualified?"

The Changed are funneling out of the refectory and scurrying off to their jobs. There are bakers, launderers, cooks, housekeepers, dairy workers, gardeners, and farmers.

"That guy was an insurance adjuster. That girl worked in McDonald's. We're two hundred years back in time here. Think he knew how to shear a sheep? Think she knew how to churn butter? But they learned. By keeping their eyes open and their mouths shut," he tells me.

"I'll nail my thumbs to the walls," I say.

Dash smirks. "Now, that would be amusing."

He walks me over to a wagon piled high with lumber.

"Brian 689, this is Thomas 2," he says to the man sitting up front. "Brian's a master carpenter. You're his apprentice."

"I don't think so," says Brian giving me the once-over. "Better look at his assignment again."

Dash reads my paperwork quickly and laughs. "Bloody hell." He claps me on the back. "My mistake," he says to Brian. He leads me to another wagon, this one loaded with equipment.

"Thomas 2, meet your boss."

The person sitting in the front of the wagon whirls around. It's Phaidra.

TWENTY-EIGHT

WE'RE SITTING IN SILENCE, DRIVING the horse and wagon to the Ministry. She sits as far away from me as she can on the wooden seat, but the ruts in the road conspire to move us closer. At times our thighs and shoulders bump up against each other and her soapy smell overwhelms me.

"So, how'd you learn carpentry?" I ask.

She doesn't bother to hide her disdain.

"I guess you learned when you got here, huh?"

Phaidra shakes her head in disgust and makes a clucking sound in the back of her throat that just about undoes me. This girl knows how to drive a team of horses and she sure as hell will know how to swing a hammer.

I try again; this time I'll appeal to her intellect.

"Is Dickens one of your favorites?"

"Oh, shut up," she says.

"Excuse me?" I say.

She pulls back on the reins so abruptly I nearly slide off the seat. The wagon jerks to a stop.

"Listen closely because I'm only going to say this once. I have no interest in babysitting you. Or becoming your friend."

"I didn't ask you to be my friend," I say, somewhat petulantly. And that's true. I don't want to be her friend: I want to kiss her, deeply, and for a long time.

She blinks slowly and I realize I was wrong about her. I had read poetry into her gaze; I had imagined her like a

November creek. She's as cold and unyielding as concrete.

"My job is to show you how to build bookshelves. That's it. I don't want to have conversations. I don't want to pretend to be interested in you. I just want to do my job and go back to the dorm," she says.

"I don't believe you. Why'd you come to Isaura if you wanted to be left alone?"

She glares at me. "I came to get away from people like you, people who get everything handed to them. People who look like they walked out of some magazine."

This is so blatantly unfair—she saw me before the Change!

"People like us, you mean?" I ask. "'Cause *you* look like *you* just stepped out of the pages of J. Crew."

God, I hate that catalog. It's the worst insult I can think of. The sad thing is most girls would have eaten it up. Not Phaidra. It infuriates her, which unfortunately makes me like her even more.

"What makes you think I've ever seen a J. Crew catalog?" she spits out.

"Well, you lived in America, didn't you?" I say.

"You're an idiot," she says.

"So they tell me," I say.

We're approaching the city. Phaidra's worked herself

up into such a state she nearly runs over a woman and her small child. In true Isaurian fashion the woman doesn't yell or scream. She simply hauls her child back onto the sidewalk until we pass.

"Lordy," I say. "Looks like you need a little practice in the horse-and-wagon department."

"You think you're better than me?" Phaidra snaps.

"What are you talking about? You saw me yesterday. You saw my face."

"I saw it, all right," she says.

"You weren't supposed to be looking at us. It's against the rules."

"I can look wherever I want. It's a free country."

I snort. "It certainly is not. We may have been fixed, but we're slaves now, in case you haven't noticed."

She shoots me a strange look out of the corner of her eye but says nothing.

Isaurians scurry around the streets, intent on their morning errands. Their beautifully woven baskets are filled with produce. Their clothes are homespun and made from vegetable dyes. At that moment I hate Isaura with a loathing only an exile can feel. Everything about the place infuriates me: its rigidity, its rules, and its stalwart refusal to move into the future.

We come around a corner, and the huge stone fortress

that is the Ministry looms in front of us. Somewhere in there is my mother's skin. I sink down in my seat, already overwhelmed and I haven't even started looking. I touch my face for comfort. It pulses beneath my fingertips like a beacon.

"Just stay out of my way," Phaidra says finally. "I've got a reputation. I'm sure Dash has already told you all about me."

"You're wrong," I say.

She raises her eyebrows in disbelief. "Well, if he hasn't, he will."

"I don't believe everything I'm told."

"You should. Everything he says about me is true. Besides, there are many girls here who are far prettier than me. Girls who will wait in line—who will go through the proper protocol in order to get a date with you," she sneers.

She makes it sound so pathetic, all those calling cards.

"I didn't ask for that," I say softly.

"Sure, you didn't, but it came your way anyway. And you didn't turn it down."

We've arrived at the Ministry. Four other carpentry wagons have beaten us there and are already unloading. Phaidra turns to me.

"Look, you're my apprentice: that doesn't mean

we're shackled to each other. Do as I ask while we're on the job and get on with the rest of your life. You'll have a good time here. Everyone seems to. All you have to do is surrender. At least that's what they tell me."

When she climbs down off the seat, I sit for a moment, trying to pull myself together. The last thing I want to do is walk into the Ministry.

"Move it," Phaidra yells.

Obediently I jump to the ground.

TWENTY-NINE

ONCE WHEN I WAS FIVE, my mother took me to work with her. I wasn't well that day. I had a fever and the sniffles. I remember walking down the long corridor, shaking with fear. My mother had warned me that the Ministry was not a place for children and that I wasn't to say a word.

Everybody seemed to be expecting us and on their best behavior. Because of my mother's high ranking they made an effort to appear friendly. Her fellow Seers said hello and chucked me on the chin. They gave me sweets and milky tea. I knew even then, at five years old, that this was not the norm, for they were a solemn bunch, and forecasting every little thing from food cravings to bowel movements so that every Isaurian would have every moment of his life pre-scripted was a solemn business.

I made the rounds with my mother that day, visiting two departments of Seers: Meals and Marriage. Now, the Marriage Seers, they were a lively bunch. I suspected that my mother, had she been less gifted and thus not relegated to predicting natural catastrophes like blizzards or hurricanes, would have settled in this department.

As soon as somebody was born, the Marriage Seers began working on finding the person a match. It could take that long because by the time they found a match, they might have had to imagine somebody's future with a thousand possible partners. But somehow they always managed to pull it off, and by the time each Isaurian came of age at eighteen, she knew who she would marry.

After visiting the Marriage Seers, we went to the Meals Department. By the time we left, I was salivating with hunger despite the fact that I had spent the last four days throwing up. Who wouldn't when all the talk was of the Murphys having a crown roast of pork on Thursday and the Lewingers having scones and clotted cream for tea next Saturday? The Meal Seers tended to be large and big bellied and they sat around a table overflowing with food, because as they forecasted everybody else's meal, they also forecast for each other. *You're having pumpkin ravioli for supper tonight. And you're to have grilled cheese and ham!* A bunch of clowns, my mother called them. She considered the Meals Department totally superfluous. Who needed to know what they would be craving a week from now? I had to agree with her. There was, however, the matter of the Changed. They needed to know, for they were the ones growing, harvesting, and preparing pretty much all of our food.

So when Phaidra and I enter the Ministry, I'm flooded with a wall of memory. Crops Room to the left. Children's Room to the right. My mother locked in her bedroom a world away.

"What wrong with you?" asks Phaidra.

"What's a crops room? Something to do with horses?" My valiant attempt at appearing ignorant.

She rolls her eyes at me.

Phaidra leads me down three corridors and up two flights of stairs and to an unmarked door. I hear hammering. The sound of wood being battered around. She raps on the door impatiently, three quick knocks, and we are let in. I look around in amazement.

"What is this place?" I ask her.

"We're building a library for a man named Otak. The High Seer of Isaura," she adds.

Some would call it luck. Others fate. Me—I'm not sure what to call it. This library? Well, it's also the antechamber to Otak's private quarters, where my mother's Seerskin is probably hidden away.

THIRTY

I SHOULD BE BESIDE MYSELF with joy that the only thing that may separate me from what I have come for is a decorative steel door. That sometime in the next few days, maybe tonight, I'll be cruising home with my mother's Seerskin tucked under my arm.

Instead what I feel is dismay. Because of my new face eight girls are coming to call on me tonight. I have to see them, right? To do otherwise would arouse suspicion.

Phaidra hands me my tools. A broom and a dustpan.

"Oh, come on," I whine, hoping nobody has seen her handing me the broom. "Give me a hammer, a saw. Something I can dig my teeth into."

She crosses her arms. "No way am I setting you loose with a saw. Besides, we're way past saws."

I look around the room. There are floor-to-ceiling bookshelves and cabinets on each of the four walls. Other workers stand on ladders, some with levels in their hands. Long maroon wood shavings litter the floor. I pick one up and sniff it.

"Cedar," I say, hoping to impress her.

"*Peltogyne paniculata*, dumbass. Purpleheart."

"Why's it called purpleheart?"

She hesitates, like I've asked her a personal question.

"It's a chameleon," she says slowly. "When the heart of the tree is exposed, it's brown. But when you slice into that heart, it turns a brilliant purple. Right before your eyes it changes color. You have to cut into it before it comes alive."

Normally I would have eaten this kind of stuff up, but something in me pulls back.

"Do you always speak about lumber in that tone of voice? Like you're talking about the Dalai Lama?" I ask her.

Her eyes widen. "Pick up the broom and get to work, Quicksilver. You won't feel so manly when you slice the tip of your finger off."

And so the morning passes and I make no attempt to get through the steel door that leads into Otak's inner sanctum. My mother has nearly three weeks left and I've decided I can afford one night here for myself with my new face. She wouldn't deny me that.

THIRTY-ONE

THERE ARE RULES THE CHANGED are expected to adhere to and I'm informed of them at lunchtime when a group of Isaurian schoolgirls strolls by.

1. *Never speak to Isaurians unless spoken to.*
2. *Relationships of any sort between Isaurians and Changed are forbidden.*
3. *Never touch an Isaurian.*

Ah, number three. The one the previous two rules are just leading up to. Bottom line: don't hook up with an Isaurian. No matter how cute she might be or how much you might be tempted. In other words, no interbreeding. Wouldn't want to dirty up the bloodline.

I nod obediently when Brian recites the rules to

me. We're sitting on a bench outside the Ministry eating our sandwiches. I'm feeling smug; these rules don't apply to me. First, because I'll be gone before anybody knows it. And second, because I'm really an Isaurian.

"Better wipe that look off your face," says Phaidra.

"Ladies first," I retort, realizing in an instant that she, too, feels smug about something. She has a secret.

The schoolgirls whisper and I look up. They're teenagers. My heart thuds as I realize chances are good I know some of them. But I've been gone for nine years. Will I recognize them? Will they recognize me? Suddenly I need to test the possibility.

I stand up so I can see better and I hear a low warning growl. Accompanying the girls is an old woman. Of course they wouldn't be unchaperoned, especially here in the city among the Changed. The woman wears the brown hooded robe of a teacher. I can't see her face—it's hidden in the shadow of her hood—but there's no mistaking her warning. She steps closer so she can see me better and I busy myself with my sandwich.

I hear Phaidra chewing methodically beside me. I glance up at her face, which is uncharacteristically vacant. I wave my hand in front of her and she smiles dimly. She lifts her hand to tuck her hair behind her ear and her shirt cuff falls to her elbow and I see that her forearm is riddled with tiny slashes. It looks like someone's taken a penknife and cut her again and again. Did Dash do this? Punishment for her insolence?

"Phaidra," I whisper, and snap my fingers.

She stares out into space

I grab her wrist and gently twist it. She gives a little screech. When she sees her arm exposed, that I've seen the crisscross of cherry-colored lines, she gasps. She yanks her sleeve down and buttons it tight around her wrist and in that instant I understand that Dash didn't do this to her; she's cut herself. But why?

"I see you're done hiding, Tom Quicksilver," a familiar voice says.

I groan silently and look up. It's Otak and this time he's not alone. He's flanked by a coterie of blue-robed Seers. You're Changed; they can't read your mind, I remind myself, but I'm filled with doubt. They look at me like they know exactly who I am and what I'm thinking. Otak leans in close to me, so close I can smell his breath, which is surprisingly fresh, and he turns my face to the left and right. I half expect him to pull my lips back and inspect my gums.

"Some of the Maker's best work," he says, letting me go.

I feel a weird combination of shame and pleasure at his comment.

He looks over his shoulder at the group of Isaurian girls.

"Rule number three, girls," he calls out.

"Never touch a Changed," they answer in unison.

But he's just touched me. That doesn't seem to occur to anybody. I stare at the girls with bewilderment. Each one holds a set of books in her arms—they must have been coming from school. Before walking off, they examine me so coldly that I feel shredded.

"Bitches," whispers Phaidra, glaring at the Isaurian girls as they sashay across the plaza.

I turn to her, surprised by this gesture of solidarity.

"Don't get all excited. A jackass is a jackass," she says. "Doesn't matter what world you're in."

THIRTY-TWO

THAT NIGHT THE GIRLS COME CALLING. There's Lina, Tammi, Trixie, Veronica, Penelope, Mee-Yon, Alex, and Mildred-I'm-changing-my-name-to-Montana.

I can't help myself. "Have you given the name Nebraska any thought?" I ask her.

"Why, no," she says. "I should have, though. I should have considered that."

She sounds just like Judy Garland, tinny and yippy, like her voice was imported from 1938.

"Certainly you toyed with Dakota?" I say.

"No," she says, blinking like she's just come out of a movie theater.

"Wyoming, then? Surely Wyoming. It's a nice place. No speed limits. Or maybe I'm confusing it with Montana. But cowboys live there. That's the important thing," I say. I pat her hand.

She smiles. She has no idea that I'm mocking her.

I am powerful for the first time in my life. I lean forward and kiss Mildred-I'm-changing-my-name-to-Montana and very quickly it no longer matters what she's changing her name to.

It's four hours later and I've had eight dates. Exactly thirty minutes with each girl. Now all I want to do is to go to sleep and replay the moment before the kiss when I have no idea how a girl's lips will taste, how her teeth will feel against my tongue, when I have no clue that her neck will smell of limes.

Tonight Montana is kind enough to show me a way out of the backwater of my inexperience, as are Lina and Trixie, and it's more than enough to make me believe in a life where anything is possible.

"You shouldn't have kissed all of them," says Dash.

"I only kissed three," I say.

"They'll talk. They'll compare notes. They won't be happy when they find out you've been with all of them," he says.

From the chirpy way they greeted each other as they passed on the porch steps, it seems unlikely to me that they'll care.

"I just told you," I say. "It was only three."

"Whatever," says Dash. "I'm going to bed."

"Wait."

"Now what?"

"I need to ask you a question."

Dash's eyes narrow. "Tomorrow."

"Tomorrow?"

"I'll take you to the infirmary. You'll get your protection, don't worry."

"Jesus!" I say.

"Look, you better get used to the attention. And you'd better figure out how to handle it. It's not going to go away," he says.

He's wrong. It *is* going to go away. My mother and her missing Seerskin come winging back into my consciousness. What kind of a sick person am I? I've been on the porch making out while my mother's on her deathbed back on Earth.

Dash eyes gaze at some spot above my head.

"You have this weird cowlick thing happening," he says.

"I do?" I reach up and pat the back of my head. There is indeed a stuck-up bristly patch.

"I can remedy that. Snip, snip. Cut it real short? Might be a better look on you anyway. You're got this polo player vibe going that honestly"—he leans forward and mock-whispers—"only works if you happen to be Argentinean." He rolls back on his heels and smirks.

"Get away from me," I say. I've always been vain about my hair. It was the only thing I had going for me before the Change.

He shrugs and turns to go.

"Wait!" Even though I've spent the evening with eight girls, suddenly I feel completely alone.

"What now?" he drawls.

"Don't go yet."

Dash looks amused, but he pulls up a chair and sits down at the table. "Sure, kid. No problem. That's my job. To babysit you."

The words are wrong, but the tone is right. There's a certain yielding in his voice. Like maybe he remembers what it was like for him when he first arrived 484 days ago.

"I don't need any babysitting," I say.

"Sure, you don't, T."

He grins softly at me in a way that reminds me of Patrick and my chin, mortifyingly, begins to wobble. My father probably lies buried under the ground not more than two miles from here. I shake my head angrily at him, trying to will my tears to stay in my eyes.

Dash looks uncomfortable at my display of emotion. "Look, just wait it out," he says gruffly. "It'll get easier. In the meantime—stop pissing people off. Stop acting like such an American. Just be a good kid."

Be a good kid. Sorry, I'd like to oblige, but I just can't. I stopped being a kid long ago, the day my face went up in flames. And as far as good—well, a good kid would not have kissed three girls practically one right after another. A good kid would not have pressed his luck and insisted on going further. He would not have let his hands travel south, past the metropolis of neck and shoulder and to the outer boroughs of rib cage and breast. But I'm starving. For life and for touch.

THIRTY-THREE

DASH GOES TO BED RIGHT after that, but I while away another couple of hours in my room. I tell myself I'm being extra safe, making sure that he's truly asleep before I sneak out of the house. But what I'm really doing is replaying the evening. I kissed a girl—I kissed three girls. I feel numb and at the same time liquefied, like I've been run through a juicer.

Finally I get my ass out the door. As I run along the forest path, I try to think only of my mother, of what I must do. I plan to go about this like a mathematician. My *Barker's* has a foldout map that shows every room in the Ministry. I have marked a quadrant, a grid that I will systematically search. Getting into the library and through the steel door to Otak's private quarters will be complicated. I'll save that for later. I need time to come up with the right plan.

That's what I tell myself, anyway.

When I get to the Ministry, I'm shocked to find there are no guards patrolling the grounds. Besides that, the building's unlocked; the place is wide open. The lack of security infuriates me even though it makes my job easier. It's just another example of Isaurian superiority and smugness. I know the way they think because I'm one of them. They don't have to lock their doors because they would know someone was coming to rob them a week before it happened. They haven't counted on me.

I enter the building. The halls are dark, but I have a candle. I light it carefully and cup the flame with my hand to dim it. I open cabinets, rummage through bookcases, and dig through drawers and I'm plagued with nostalgia again.

I was happy here. I walked these halls every day for eight years. I loved the simplicity and the rigidity of our lives, because I didn't know anything else. I'll say one thing for Isaura: I always felt safe here. Until my parents were flayed of their skins, that is.

I only manage to get through two rooms, because it takes a decidedly long time to do a thorough search. I have to paw through the most mundane and quotidian of items: ancient, musty robes, sheaves of paper, and an entire cabinet filled with nothing but empty picture frames. Finally I blow out the candle and stand in the corridor. This is going to take some time, I realize. And I wonder why I'm not feeling any sense of panic.

THIRTY-FOUR

ONCE AGAIN I'M LATE FOR breakfast. I hurry from the house, trying to dodge the huge pellets of rain. This morning I am Thomas 9.

The days are bleeding into one another: a blur of carpentry, girls, and nights spent searching the Ministry for my mother's Seerskin. Well, that's not completely accu-rate. I haven't searched *every* night.

This morning I can't get to the Refectory fast enough. I need my fix. Not of eggs or sausage, but of attention. I crave the gaze of others like I crave water.

I push my plate away, aware that people are watch-ing and that their watching is beyond their control: my face requires it of them; it commands them to. Under their eyes I become something outside myself. I have to be disassembled in order to be understood. The curve of my jaw, the arch of my eyebrows, the way my hair falls onto my forehead.

Somebody tugs on my shirt.

"Don't forget about tonight." It's Emma.

"Tonight?"

"We're meeting for dinner, remember?"

"Oh yeah." I can't hide my disappointment. The last thing I want to do is have dinner with my group. But it's required. All groups must meet once a week. I glance over at the table where the rest of them are sitting. They're rarely apart. Michael looks up at me sourly. He has elected himself foreman, and our dislike of each other has grown. The sight of him makes me feel like I have a noose around my neck. I have no time for him or for my group. I'm running the race of my life, to live every moment I can with this face before it's taken away from me, but I can't tell them that.

Rose gives a little wave. The twins are busy shoveling food into their mouths.

"Yeah, whatever," I say.

Emma smirks at me. "Michael said there was a snowball's chance in hell of you coming."

Michael. He's beginning to become a problem. I get up, put my arm around Emma, and walk over to their table. "See you tonight," I say, trying to sound chipper.

"Gonna grace us with your presence?" asks Michael.

"Michael," cautions Rose.

"No. Someone's got to say it." He stands up, puts both palms flat on the table, and leans forward. "I don't know what game you're playing, son, but it's getting tiresome. At least pretend you think there's somebody else in this world besides yourself."

"Sir, yes, sir." I clack my heels together.

He glowers at me. "Perhaps you could be a bit more creative. Or has your face eaten up your brain?"

A spasm of fury sets my jaw twitching.

"Just come," says Rose.

"I said I would," I snarl.

"All right, then." Rose turns to Michael as if he doesn't speak the language and she has to translate for him. "Thomas is coming." She looks out the window. "Shall we go out and get some fresh air?"

After they leave, Jerome turns to me and asks, "What's got into you?"

"Listen, I already have enough people telling me what to do."

Jerome throws up his hands. "Not the enemy."

"But Michael . . . he's just—" I say.

"He's not so bad," interrupts Jerome. "If you spent any time with us, you'd know that."

"He's a dick," I say.

Jerome stands up. "Don't bother coming tonight."

"Fine. Whatever you want."

He looks at me with disgust. "It's not what I want. It's what *you* want. But that's the point, isn't it? You get whatever you want now, right?"

"Well, don't you think it's time? Don't you feel the same way? That you should get every damn thing you missed out on, every single minute of your life that you spent suctioned on to your brother's rib cage; that it should all be given back to you to do over? Come on. Aren't you angry? The least little bit?" I bait him.

Jerome wipes my spit off his cheek. "No. I'm not angry. I'm grateful," he says softly.

I don't show up for dinner that night. Or the next night either.

THIRTY-FIVE

PHAIDRA TUCKS HER TAPE MEASURE back into her tool belt, hefts the plank over her shoulder, and carries it into the hallway. Her competence dizzies me. She's nothing like the girls who make up my fan club. I have begun thinking of them as a collective: "the Connecticuts," I secretly call them.

The Connecticuts are pleasant and easy to please and they adore me. They are bejeweled rivers that may rise above their banks but will never flood. And they are interchangeable.

So if Lina, Tammi, Trixie, Veronica, Penelope, Mee-Yon, Alex, and Mildred-I'm-changing-my-name-to-Montana are the Connecticuts, then what does that make Phaidra? Phaidra, who would sooner saw off her arm than assimilate into the Changed community. I think I should file her under the oft-maligned New Jersey—a misunderstood and underappreciated state.

I like New Jersey and think of it fondly, in much the way someone would think of a crackpot uncle. I went with Patrick and his mother once to the Jersey Shore. I remember some rinky-dink boardwalk. Eating fried dough. The icy greenness of the aloe vera gel Clara spread on our sunburned backs at night.

For the first time since I've gotten here, I find myself alone in the half-finished Ministry library. Everyone else has gone out for lunch. Finally I've got an opportunity to search Otak's private quarters. The steel door has been haunting me. I've dreamed about it; the bronze curlicues strangling me in the night.

I see a flash of color and movement and Brian stands beside me. He has a habit of suddenly appearing out of nowhere, like a roadrunner. He takes a swig from his canteen and wipes his chin with the back of his hand.

"You coming?" he asks.

"In a minute." I heft the broom, indicating I've got more sweeping to do.

"I'll save you a sandwich," he says, and leaves.

I like Brian. He's serene. Occasionally a bit of his dry wit surfaces, but mostly he does his job and goes home. I try to stir him up now and then, hide his hammer, drop a wood shaving into his soup, but he is unruffleable.

It's the same with most of the Changed who have been here awhile. Dash said things would get easier after the first hundred days. And it really does seem to be the case. But there's something about Brian's tranquility that bothers me. He's nice but disturbingly remote. Same with the Connecticuts, who let me touch them wherever I want but whose personalities, it occurs to me now, are like distant islands glimpsed through the fog of a winter dawn.

But not Phaidra. She is still sharp, hard, blindingly bright. Why is she different?

A thought bubbles up: none of this will matter in a few days, once I find my mother's Seerskin. And suddenly I feel like I weigh a thousand pounds.

I wait a moment to be sure Brian is gone and then I open Otak's door.

THIRTY-SIX

HERE IT IS, THE OLD man's bed. I find it a grotesquely intimate sight, like seeing a pair of discarded underwear on a city street. It's a massive piece of furniture, a fortress, really; the headboard is one single length of wood. I want to dirty it somehow, penetrate its invincibility. I fight off the urge to lie down. Oh, what the hell.

I press my face into the pillows; they smell of bleach and lavender soap. I lean over and riffle through the top drawer of his bedside table. I do not find my mother's Seerskin; I find a candle stub and five cherry candies.

Suddenly there's a loud rattling. Startled, I hurl myself off the bed and onto my feet. A bird has flown into the window. It remains glued to the glass for a moment. Its obsidian eyes look at me with a disturbingly human gaze before it slides off. I swear I see its claws steepled together as if in prayer.

"Crashing into the window rarely kills them. It's the twenty-foot drop that does them in. Most of their bones are hollow, you know." Otak stands in the doorway, a toothpick wedged between his teeth. "Have you lost your way?" he asks me pleasantly.

What I have lost is my ability to speak. In his private quarters Otak appears to have grown to twice his normal size. I understand why he needs such a large bed to accommodate him. His gnarled, yellowed hands are as big as lions' heads.

"Tommy, is it?" He looks at me with interest, his head cocked. It seems all I've done since the moment I arrived is to draw attention to myself.

"Tom," I say.

"Tom, yes. Are you in search of something, Tom?"

Yes, indeed, Otak. You son of a bitch.

"There you are!" Phaidra storms into the room. She seizes my wrist. "What's wrong with you? Can't you follow simple directions? I told you the supply room was down the hall and to the right." She bobs to Otak. "I'm sorry. He's only just arrived." She wrenches me across the parquet floor.

"Oh no, you must stay," he says, picking up a little bell and ringing it. A maid appears. "Ah, Roberta. Tea. Fennel for me. And peppermint for my young friends. And bring me my pipe." Roberta retrieves the pipe; Otak lights it and waves his hand at us. "Come, sit."

Phaidra gives me a stunned look as we follow the High Seer of Isaura to his parlor. The couches are overstuffed and smell of eucalyptus. All the furniture is varying shades of blue.

"You are a carpenter?" he asks Phaidra.

"Yes."

Otak eyes her tool belt. "You did not do this in your world."

"Right." Her voice surrenders nothing. I love this about her and think it's the most foolish damn thing, given our present circumstances.

"And you?"

I feel ashamed. I want to say I'm a carpenter too, but my broom is propped up against Otak's bedroom wall. "I'm her apprentice," I say.

"He's only been here ten days," says Phaidra.

I can't believe she's defending me. I don't dare look over at her.

"You're saying he'll better himself?"

"Yes. I think he's got potential."

I feel like a three-year-old whose parents are talking about him as if he's not there while he's in the room.

"What's your name?" Otak asks.

"Phaidra," she tells him.

The scent of Otak's tobacco is cloying, dark red and moist, like the inside of a cave or a Black Forest cake. I glance over at Phaidra. She has fallen down into the pillows of the couch. She tries to rearrange her limbs, but the cushions are too deep. She looks like she is drowning. I sit up erect in response to her slumping.

"Do you mind if I examine you?" Otak asks Phaidra.

"I'd prefer it if you didn't," she says.

"It was not really a question," he says.

Phaidra shakes her head vehemently and fear flashes across her face.

"Come here," he says.

She doesn't move.

"Now," he says firmly.

He is the High Seer of Isaura; she gets up and stands in front of him.

"You have been here how many days?" he inquires.

"A hundred and ten, a hundred and twelve?" he guesses.

"One hundred and thirteen," says Phaidra stonily.

Otak studies her face carefully. "One hundred and thirteen days; I see. Yet you seem dissatisfied somehow," he says, almost gently. "Aren't you pleased with what we've done for you?"

Phaidra tugs on her shirtsleeves, nervously pulling down the cuffs. She doesn't want him to see that she's cutting into her flesh. That's when I realize: that's why she does it. Somehow it keeps her fierce. It keeps her from floating away internally, like one of the Connecticuts.

She shoots me a frantic look, like there's a fire on the prairie and the flames are licking her jackrabbity feet. Adrenaline races through me. If he hurts her, I will kill him. I will throw him out the window and then we'll see if his bones are as hollow as the bird's.

But he doesn't hurt her. Instead he asks, "What was wrong with you?"

Confusion closes Phaidra's face like a shutter. She looks at me sideways.

"Oh, of course," says Otak. "Not in front of the boy. Well, whisper it to me, then."

I feel a sudden wave of jealousy. Don't fall for it, I

think, but it's too late: she's telling him her secrets and I understand why. He's making Phaidra feel like he's terribly interested in hearing her story. *He doesn't care,* I want to yell at her. *It's all an act.* Isn't it?

"That's horrible," he says when she's done.

His voice is not riddled with compassion, but something simple and bright that doesn't pretend to be anything other than what it is—the truth. And I'm filled with longing. How I yearn for fact, how I crave accuracy and precision—it's the Isaurian in me.

Otak is seducing us with the truth. Adults rarely take this tack with teenagers. They don't know how they could reel us in, how they could make us do whatever they wanted if only they told us the truth. Otak's right. Whatever happened to Phaidra, whatever she was, whatever life she had to live in her old failing body was without a doubt horrible.

It's at this moment that I realize I am in trouble. I miss this life, my old life in Isaura. And what if, when the time I have left here is up, I can't find my mother's Seerskin? Then what? If I don't have my mother to worry about any longer, if there's nothing I can do to prevent her dying, if I have no pressing reason to go back to Earth, can I surrender to the Change?

And stay?

THIRTY-SEVEN

"YOU LITTLE SHIT," SAYS PHAIDRA when we finally make it back to the library two hours later. It's nearly six. Everybody has already left. Because of me we have a long walk back to the Compound.

"That's Mr. Shit to you," I say. Because of me our bellies are full of orange scones and peppermint tea, but I don't mention this.

She shakes her head. Once again I've managed to underwhelm her with my witty repartee. Phaidra scowls and begins to jog down the corridor.

"No running inside the Ministry," I shout, picking up my pace to catch up with her.

"What are you, five? You think anybody cares?"

"I do. I think they care a great deal," I say, huffing to keep up with her. She's in good shape. I might not beat her in a race. This pleases and annoys me. I keep thinking I've gotten myself free of wanting her; then she sucks me back in with her tractor beam of indifference.

It feels good to run. Good to sweat. We canter out of the city and into the woods. I feel so utterly strong and Paul Bunyan–ish, running with this spectacularly beautiful and rakishly intelligent girl by my side, that I can actually imagine wringing the trees with my bare hands and squeezing the sap into our mouths.

"Did you run track?" I pant at her.

"No. Christ." She stops suddenly and looks at me. "I have absolutely no idea why I came after you, Quicksilver."

She's wearing a ponytail. The strands closest to her neck are wet with sweat. I would like to place my lips at the place where her backbone begins. At the little knob that juts out like a drawer pull.

"What were you doing in his bedroom?" she fires at me.

"I just wanted to see what the passageway led to," I say.

"No. You're after something."

"Everybody's after something," I say.

She shakes her head at me; she's not buying it.

"You do a great deal of head shaking," I tell her. "Has anybody ever told you that?"

She gives me a withering look.

"Ow," I say.

"You're a real piece of work," she says.

"So why did you come after me?" I ask.

I have a theory. I think she likes me but doesn't want to admit it because she doesn't want to like anybody in

Isaura because that would mean she wants to stay. And I don't think she wants to stay. She wants to stay in her new body, but she does *not* want to stay in Isaura.

"Because you're my apprentice, you ass," she says. "I'm responsible for you. Whatever you do reflects badly on me. If you don't get trained, *I'm* in trouble."

"It's more than that," I say.

I want to wrest the truth from her. All this combustion between us. It has to mean something.

"I like you," I say softly.

Her eyes narrow with suspicion.

"No, I mean I really *like* you, Phaidra."

"I see," she says. "Like you like Trixie?"

I blunder on, suddenly desperate to prove my worthiness to her despite having been with so many girls that I don't care about. That's not who I am. I need her to know that.

"You don't see things the way most people do," I say. "You're so . . . fearless."

Phaidra's face hardens. "I'm not fearless," she says.

"Of course you're not. That's not what I meant. That you're a robot or something," I say stupidly.

Phaidra glowers at me in silence.

"Your name," I say quickly, trying to salvage the conversation. "Is it Greek?"

Phaidra shakes her head. "You don't need to know the derivation of my name. Stop acting like this is going somewhere. I don't feel the same way about you."

"What way?" I ask.

Phaidra wheels around. "God, you're relentless," she cries, her hands on her hips. "All right. Here it is. I have no feelings for you whatsoever. None. I don't care about you; I don't care what happens to you. Get it?"

"Oh," I say in the smallest of voices, bile rushing up into my throat.

She glares at me, her cheeks flushed pink. "You pushed us here," she says.

"Yes, I'm an idiot," I say.

She doesn't disagree with me. I struggle to regain my composure, but it's useless. I'm utterly vulnerable and I can't hide it. I just look at her miserably.

Phaidra runs off. My feet feel like they're encased in blocks of concrete.

What do I do? Go after her? Try to make her fall in love with me when I know I'm leaving any day?

Nothing is clear anymore.

Phaidra's right: I am relentless. At least, as a child I was. I used to test my mother constantly. There was a part of me that suspected she loved me more than my father. And if I wasn't right about that, if she didn't love me more than him, then certainly she loved me in a different way, without guile, without restriction. I was dependent on her. Under her gaze, and only her gaze, I became three-dimensional; I sprang to life.

But now my mother is depending on me and there's a chance that I'm going to let her down. Would she want me to stay and make a life here, in the world where I was born? Would she deny me the birthright of a normal face? No, I don't think she would. Not the mother I grew up with. Not the mother she used to be before she got so sick.

Entertaining these thoughts makes my throat ache violently. The tears come fast now, blurring my vision. I cram my fist against my mouth to keep myself from crying out.

THIRTY-EIGHT

"YOU'RE COMING ALONG NICELY," SAYS Dash late that night. "Keep this up and you may get to leave Orientation early."

He's referring to the fact that I've just spent the evening with two of the Connecticuts: Veronica and Mee-Yon. For some reason, Dash believes there's some correlation between dating and my successful assimilation into the Changed community. He thinks all this attention from the opposite sex will result in my conversion.

He's wrong. The more time I spend with the Connecticuts, the more they weird me out. They are the strangest girls I've ever met. They don't seem to mind that I see one of them right after the other. On the contrary: tonight, after an hour had passed, Veronica got up of her own volition and left the porch seat vacant for Mee-Yon as if some internal bell had gone off. I even heard them saying a cordial hello to each other in the dark as they passed on the street. Mee-Yon's only concession to being preempted by Veronica was that she asked me to wipe my mouth with a napkin before I kissed her. I obliged, of course, for I was living a boy's dream, wasn't I?

They're beginning to wear on me. More than once I've wanted to grab the Connecticuts by their collective shoulders and shake them. But I don't, because each one of them gives me her undivided fawning attention and I've become a junkie—if I don't get my daily hit, I go into withdrawal.

Meanwhile Dash and I have found some way to manage. He uses the outhouse first in the morning; I put the kettle on for tea. I don't bore him with my carpentry mishaps; he doesn't come to me for conversation. We are professional.

Neither of us wants a repeat of that night when I offered him my Levi's.

"So how's Ms. Master Carpenter?" asks Dash casually.

He's trying to act nonchalant, like he's inquiring about the weather, but I know he's got a thing for Phaidra and he wants news. *Anything.* Is she wearing her hair a different way? Does her skin smell of lemon or turpentine? I give him the truth.

"She sucks," I say. "She treats me like the dog shit she scraped from the bottom of her shoe last week."

Dash's eyes recede in his head and he guffaws. Here's something he didn't expect from me. Bravado, yes. Bluster and arrogance. But not self-deprecation. It's a relief for us both.

I know my willfulness drives Dash crazy. I feel sorry for him, but not too bad. In exchange for babysitting me he gets all sorts of extras, like cigarettes and whiskey.

"Is it worth it?" I ask, gesturing to the pack of Marlboros sitting on the table.

His eyes narrow. "You just don't know when to quit, do you?"

"I wish I could quit," I say.

He studies me. "You don't wish any such thing, loser," he says.

THIRTY-NINE

At breakfast the next morning I'm informed that I have once again forgotten to attend our group meeting. This makes two missed meetings in a row. Michael tells me I've left him no choice: he will have to tell my Host.

"You do that," I say to his retreating back as he self-importantly, and may I add eagerly, marches up to their table to report me.

Dash storms up and slams his fist down on the table, sending the silverware flying. "Think you're better than everyone else? Think the rules don't apply to you, Thomas 11?" he hollers.

"You knew where I was," I remind him.

"I didn't know you were supposed to be somewhere else," he says.

Emma cups my elbow protectively. She's developed a crush on me and her adoration unmoors me. It's like an extravagantly watered lawn, so green it hurts to look at it. She nestles into my hip. I push her away. She emits a tiny cry of protest.

"Thomas," she insists, "pay attention to me."

"Not now, Emma," I say.

Her eyes widen with desperation. "I—I need to tell you something," she stammers.

"And I said *later*. Are you deaf?"

"What's wrong with you!" Rose grabs me by the arm and whirls me around.

"There's nothing wrong with him," says Trixie, grabbing my other arm. I push them both away, only to have Emma creep back and take my hand. Her flesh is dimpled and soft; even though she's eleven, she's still got her baby fat.

"It's all right," she whispers. "Everyone forgets. I forgive you."

Did her parents take her disease out on her? Did they hate her for making them live in the dark? Did they resent having to live an upside-down life where night was day and day was night? And did she apologize like this to them? Did she forgive them for hating her?

I give her hand a squeeze and she squeezes back.

"I'm a jerk," I say.

"Yup," she agrees. She has been in the sun constantly. Her skin's turned the color of wheat.

"I'm sorry I missed the meeting," I tell her.

"It's okay. You can come next week," she says.

"You *better* go," says Dash.

All of a sudden somebody cries out, "Something's wrong with Geld!"

The old man has gone rigid in his chair. It looks like somebody has stuck a pole through him.

"How long has he been here?" asks Rose.

"Thirty-two thousand, seven hundred and ninety-six days," answers Jesse.

Geld begins to shake. He's wrapped up in a shawl, but his bald head is bare. "I was a double amputee!" he shouts.

Nancy, the Head Host, strides across the Refectory floor. "Quiet, nobody wants to hear that," she says. She looks down at his writhing body, evaluating him. She tells Dash to go to the infirmary and get the Compound nurse.

Panic spreads across Geld's face. "No," he gasps. The spasms intensify, shaking him out of his chair and onto the floor. "Let me . . . go."

Nancy squats by him and assesses the situation coolly. I know she's thinking only about herself. How much trouble will she get in if she lets him have his way?

"Please," Geld begs. He grabs Nancy's wrist and she recoils. "There's nothing left."

I remember the first time I saw Geld. How everybody, including myself, had the urge to talk right over him, pretend he wasn't there. If the Connecticuts are remote islands, Geld is no more than a nubbin of coral, worn down so far that it no longer ruffles the surface of the sea. Long before this day, he was just *gone*.

Is it because of the Change? Does it gradually leach away the thing that makes us human?

I stare at Geld lying there on the floor, still now. He reminds me of the bird that creamed itself against Otak's window, the way it gave up, just slid right off the glass, knowing it would fall twenty feet to the ground.

"Get him help!" yells Phaidra.

Dash shakes his head, a look of fury on his face. He crosses the room and I trail after him like a little kid.

Dash helps Geld straighten his limbs, makes him comfortable on the floor. "You go now," he tells Geld. "It's all right. I won't let them bring you back."

"Thank you," says Geld. It's the last thing he says before he withers away. It's like somebody suctions the air out of him and within moments he is a husk. All at once everyone begins talking as if it never happened. As if they've forgotten they just watched a man die in front of them.

Everyone except for Phaidra; she runs from the Refectory. I want to follow her. But I just stand there because like everybody else, I'm partly relieved he's gone.

I don't go out that night to search for my mother's Seerskin. I'm so agitated over the morning's events that I make myself sick. Dash summons the Compound nurse and she gives me something to help me sleep. He sits in the room with me as I drift off. I'd like to think it's because he cares for me, but I know he's just doing his job. It's his responsibility to make sure I make it through the first hundred days intact.

As I'm drifting off, I forget where I am. Time collapses and I think I'm at Cook's house just after the fire, my seeping eyes covered in gauze. I writhe around on the mattress "My Barker's," I say.

Dash's face is blurry; it looms large and then it retracts.

"Where'd you leave it, T?" he whispers.

"In the outhouse," I say. "In the lime."

When I open my eyes shortly before dawn the next morning, the book is perched on top of my boots.

FORTY

THAT DASH HAS FOUND MY primer is not a good thing, but I'm not sure what I can do about it. I hope he'll come to the obvious conclusion: that I've stolen the book from the Ministry. I am working in the library, after all. That's not so bad, I tell myself. So he thinks

I'm a thief. Far better than him figuring out the truth.

I remain in my room obsessing until daylight, then I leave in search of distraction. I go to Trixie's dorm. I grab a handful of pebbles and throw them at her window. Moments later she comes tiptoeing out in her nightgown.

"Hello, Thomas 12," she says.

Trixie has short blond hair; she's sturdy and rosy cheeked; she looks like Nancy Drew.

I take her to the barn. It's like every bad movie you've ever seen. We fall into a pile of hay. Let me tell you something about hay. It's no good. It's scratchy and it makes you sneeze. But where else are two teenagers to go?

"Don't you want to touch me?" Trixie finally asks after we've been lying there for about ten minutes.

"Yes," I say.

But I'm not sure. In theory I do. But here's what happens: suddenly I become discriminating. I don't want to feel just any old breast. I want the breast to belong to somebody I have feelings for. Trixie's not a romantic. She takes my hand and slips it into her nightgown anyway. I rest my fingers on her neck, killing time. I pretend her collarbone is a keyboard. I play it like I'm Scott Joplin performing the "Maple Leaf Rag."

"Come on," she says.

I retract my hand. "Not today."

"You changed your mind?"

"I'm sorry." Trixie is a beautiful girl. I can't believe I'm turning her down.

She buttons up her nightgown. "You like Veronica better?" This is said with very little affect, like she might have been commenting on this year's crop of tomatoes.

"No. It's not like that," I say.

"Tammi?"

"No, not her either."

She fixes her gaze on me. Her lashes are so pale blond they appear white. She shakes her head. "I don't understand."

"I don't understand either," I say.

We walk out of the barn together. I pluck hay off the sleeve of her nightgown. It's going to be another perfect day. The sky is cloudless. The sun has just risen above the trees. Suddenly I feel despair. I see Geld writhing around on the floor, pleading with Nancy to let him die. I see this beautiful girl offering me her breasts and me not really caring. And I see Phaidra.

She's got a book tucked under her arm; in her hand she holds a steaming mug of tea. She's on her way somewhere. We've obviously interrupted her.

Phaidra shoots me a look of disgust and tries to stuff the book under her sweater.

Trixie stops and surveys Phaidra. "She hates you," she tells me.

"Yup," I say. My hair is sticking up in the back. Flattened from lying in the hay.

"See ya." Trixie lopes off to the right.

Phaidra shakes her head in disbelief.

"Are you going or coming?" I call out cheerfully, intent on ignoring the fact that I've just been spotted coming out of the barn with a girl covered in hay.

"Sleaze," she snarls, and stalks off in a westerly direction. I follow her.

"You're welcome to your opinion," I say.

"It's not opinion. It's fact. Everybody knows it."

"Well, if everybody knows it, I'd prefer you call me a cad. It's a classier word, don't you think?"

She hoots. "Okay, Mr. Darcy."

I'm determined not to swear. She's winding her way through the woods and it's all I can do to keep up with her.

"What are you reading?" I call out. I want her to know I've seen the book.

She begins running, trying to lose me. She tosses her tea into the air. Beads of golden liquid hang suspended in the turquoise sky. I pound after her. We wend our way over roots; we clamber over huge boulders of granite. I smell mica. I smell wild onion. This girl . . . *this girl*.

Suddenly she stops short and spins around. She hurls her mug at me. I jump out of the way, but I'm too late. It hits me on the bridge of the nose and when I land on my feet, I land all wrong. My leg twists beneath me and I hear the bone cracking.

The agony is a train. It's slow to come, but I know it's on its way. I can see its headlights ahead, but it's far away, just creeping, creeping. All at once it pulls into the station and I'm bathed in the screeching of the wheels, in the smell of engine and grease.

I give a long drawn-out "Fuckkkkk." I knew the moratorium on cursing wouldn't last long. I jam my fist in my mouth, hard. One pain to take away the other.

"It's your fault!" she screams.

I don't answer her. I'm afraid I'll pass out.

"Why don't you just leave me alone!" she says.

"I'm afraid I can't do that," I say.

And then she's kneeling beside me and she's cupping my head in her hands like it's a chalice and I'm saying foppish, melodramatic things like, "Shoot me," and she's saying, "No, no, no. Lie very still. Don't leave, Thomas. Don't leave."

But I do.

FORTY-ONE

"T HOMAS . . ."

When I come to, Alice, the Maker, is peering down at me. Pain undulates through me and I toss my head back like a horse and groan.

"Relax, Quicksilver."

It's Dash. I feel unduly happy at hearing his voice. This is what trauma does to a person.

"I'm going to Change you now," Alice says.

I struggle to sit up. I want to puke. I'm going to be punished. She's going to take back my face.

"No, your leg, not your face," says Alice. I see my leg twisted beneath me at an unnatural angle and she presses her hand gently against my chest, lowering my torso back down to the ground. As soon as she touches me, the last hour begin to rewind. She doesn't have to tell me to surrender this time, to let her in. I want her to take it all back. I thrust the previous sixty-two minutes at her like I'm pushing a coat into her arms.

She finds the exact moment when my tibia cracks and, like Helen Keller, blindly but with utter faith, fingers it down the middle. She's a trafficker in possibility. It's a seam she's after, for every moment can go one of two ways, and now she must convince the moment to rethink itself, to move in a different direction. She massages the seam. She steams it open with her intention. And as she does this, slowly my pain begins to dissipate. It's such a relief to feel it lift that I want to tell her I love her. And I do. I'm filled with gratitude. Luckily she's a professional; she pretends she doesn't hear me.

"You're done," she says.

Dash hauls me to my feet. I gingerly test the leg. I put my full weight on it. I bounce from foot to foot and give a triumphant cry.

"You're such a loser," says Dash.

I don't disagree with him this time. I glance over at Phaidra. To get me help, she must have run to the Ministry and back without stopping. Her cheeks are punch red and I think she's trembling. Or maybe that's me. Everything appears to be quivering.

"Sorry to have disturbed you," says Dash to Alice.

"It's all right. I was just reading." Alice gives me a searching look.

"Anything good?" I ask her.

She studies me solemnly for a moment. It's hard to remember that we're the same age. She has such poise.

"It's a book about a woman who throws herself in front of a train," she says.

Phaidra's head shoots up.

"She does something wrong. She has to make amends; she has to unmake what she's done," continues Alice.

This sounds familiar. This sounds like *Anna Karenina*. Suddenly I remember the tiny library my mother brought me to the day before the fire, the one filled with books from Earth. I had pulled out *Anna Karenina* that day and now the Maker is talking about that very book. Earth books are forbidden in Isaura. Alice has no business reading them. What's going on?

"Do you like it?" I ask cautiously.

"I can't put it down," Alice says. Then abruptly she leaves.

Dash turns to me. He's no bookworm; no chance he recognizes Tolstoy's masterpiece. "No work today, either of you. You go back to the house and rest. Phaidra, go back to the dorms." He squints into the sun, watching Alice climb back up the hill. "I better make sure she gets back to the Ministry okay." He jogs after her.

Once they're out of sight, Phaidra turns to me and says with urgency, "She was trying to tell us something."

In the aftermath of pain, I'm so tired I can barely speak. I don't know how I'll make it back to the house.

"Anna Karenina," she says.

I nod. So Phaidra had figured it out too.

She walks across the clearing and dips down. She rustles

through a pile of leaves and retrieves the book she was carrying. *Anna Karenina*—the title's embossed in gold on the spine. "How did she know?" she demands.

"Where did you get this?" I ask.

Phaidra frowns. "Does it matter?"

"Yes, it matters," I say.

"I found it," she says.

"Where?"

"In the Refectory."

She's lying. I know she stole it from the library in the Ministry. But I don't push her. Ah, my little Phaidra is a thief. This makes me like her even more. Admiration surges through me, making me feel drunk. I wobble and clutch at her arm. Even though Alice has fixed my leg, I'm still weak. Or maybe I just want an excuse to touch her.

She lets me put my arm around her shoulders and I lean into her. We walk slowly up the hill. I try not to sweat, but it's nearly impossible. It's electrifying being so near her.

"You're not getting it, Quicksilver. She's read it too. She's breaking the rules by reading a book from Earth and she wants us to know about it."

I do get it. This is what my mother did too. Reading the literature from Earth was the first step in my mother's rebellion, in her realization that she might be missing out by living in a world where every moment was prescribed and predicted.

We finally make it to the crest of the hill and the Compound sprawls out before us. I can see the green; Dash's tidy house is on the other side of it. I long for bed. I also long to extend this moment; I finally have Phaidra in my arms—or rather, I'm in her arms. It's not how I imagined it, but here we are anyway.

Phaidra lets go of me suddenly. "I hate this place," she cries.

"Me too," I say weakly, wanting to align myself with her.

"Liar!" Phaidra wheels around to face me; her features are contorted with rage.

"What did I do?" I ask.

"Exactly! You've done nothing. How can you not have questioned all this? You think they gave you this face for free?" She pokes me hard in the chest. "Don't you feel something leaking? Some essential part of you?"

I shrug.

"You're so easy," she says.

"I'm not easy!" I say. I'm tired of her insulting me.

"Then work! Don't let them take the old you away. It was valuable. Maybe the thing that made you most alive. Look at Geld. That's our future. Stay here long enough and you'll become transparent. A ghost. Every day you lose a bit of yourself. Look at your fan club. They're interchangeable, aren't they? They're beautiful, but so what? There's nothing left inside. Nothing compelling. Nothing unique. Let me tell you something. The first one hundred days? The leaking has already begun, but you don't know it yet. It's happening somewhere deep inside you. Below the skin, below the muscle, behind the heart. But make no mistake. You're bleeding out your life. Don't tell me you can't feel it."

Hearing what I've already guessed makes me perversely angry at her. "So let me guess. You've got a solution," I say.

She glares at me. "Yeah, I've got a solution. Resist!"

"Uh-huh. And how do you do that? By slicing yourself open?" I yank up her sleeve and she cries out. There's a deep gash on the pale flesh of her forearm. It's raw and ugly.

She wrenches her arm back. "Don't! That's private. That's none of your business!"

"Then why don't you make it my business?" I challenge her.

"Because you're too busy with Trixie and Veronica and you like having the life sucked out of you. I can see that you do. You want to be all serene and tranquil."

Suddenly I'm exhausted. "What's wrong with tranquil?" I ask.

She glares at me. "You can't be serious. You're seventeen years old. You're not supposed to be tranquil. You're supposed to be lit all the time. A fire raging inside you."

"I've been on fire. It's overrated."

"That's so sad," she says. "You can't stop making jokes. I feel sorry for you."

"Don't pity me," I snap.

"But I do. I saw what you looked like."

I can't stand that she saw me before I was Changed. "You saw nothing," I whisper hoarsely.

"I see everything. And I'm fighting to retain it. And you have to too," she cries.

I look down at my feet. Minutes pass. The silence engulfs us. I'm overwhelmed: seeing Phaidra's arm sliced open, breaking my leg, my futile search for my mother's Seerskin. I don't want to cry in front of her. Not again. But she places her hands on my shoulders and I can't help it; a moan escapes.

"Don't you see, Thomas? Alice wanted us to know she's on our side," says Phaidra.

Just to hear her say my name—

"On the side of what?" I whisper.

"Of this." She leans in and touches her lips lightly to mine.

I look at her in shock. "I thought you didn't like me," I say.

"I don't like you, Quicksilver," she says softly. "I haven't liked you from the first moment I laid eyes on you." She leans in and kisses me again.

There is a kiss. One kiss that is earmarked as yours the very moment you are born. It's out there waiting for you and every day that passes, every week, every month, you inch closer to that kiss. And when it's finally in sight after all those years, you run. You race toward it like it's life itself.

· PART ·
THREE

FORTY-TWO

I'M STANDING AT THE TOP of a ladder outside the Ministry. I'm washing windows, but I don't mind. Yesterday Phaidra kissed me and this morning I feel more clearheaded than ever. I *will* find my mother's Seerskin. I've searched through fifteen rooms in the Ministry; only eleven left to go.

"Are you handy, boy?"

I swivel around. There's that old woman again, the teacher, standing below me on the cobblestones. Her brown robes are now a familiar sight. Every day she appears in the city square with her charges, a long strand of girls extending behind her like a beaded neck-lace. She seems to have nothing better to do than watch us do our jobs.

"No," I answer truthfully.

"Come down from there," she says. This is the first time she's spoken to me.

I climb down off the ladder. I can't see her face. She always wears her hood, no matter what the weather.

She looks around carefully before speaking. There's no reason for her to be consulting with me, never mind interrupting my work. "If you're not handy, what are you?" she asks.

This is a strange question. It sounds disturbingly like a riddle.

"I'm not sure what you mean," I say blandly, in a tone that's meant to both deflect attention and send her on her way.

The girls titter; they cup their mouths with their small hands so as not to make any sound. She dispatches them to the fountain in the middle of the plaza. They sit in a neat row, their backs to the water.

"What's your name?" she whispers.

"Thomas."

I hear a small gasp. She clears her throat.

"Thomas what?"

"Thomas 13."

"I see. And why are you here, Thomas 13?"

Her eyes glimmer beneath the hood; they are a vivid, oceanic blue. I start to feel slightly dizzy, pulled into her orbit. Is she a Seer? Is this some sort of a test?

"I'm not supposed to say."

"You must tell me," she says.

"I can't."

"Then I'll guess."

I glance up at the window, wishing Phaidra or Brian would come rescue me from this bizarre old woman.

"Let's see," she says softly. "You were sitting in the sink. You were confused. You pulled the curtains down on top of yourself. When it burned, the fabric smelled sweet, like buttery pecans." She tilts her head to the side like a wren, considering me.

I gaze at her in shock.

"You thought you heard the sound of a wagon. Horses. You thought somebody was coming to save you." She slowly pulls back her hood. "Me."

I'm staring into the creased face of my beloved Cook. She looks like she's aged twenty years, but it's her.

"You left without saying goodbye," I gasp. Suddenly I'm eight years old.

"I didn't leave—you did. That was your mother's doing." Cook snaps her hood back up. "People are watching, Thomas Gale. You must be very careful."

I nod. Her charges are getting restless. She glances behind her and with one withering look reduces them to silence. They are en route to a puppet show. There will be no fighting, no scrambling around for seats, because it was already predetermined a week ago just exactly where each girl would sit.

"Twelve Dunny Road, do you remember? Tell them I'm in need of some new pantry shelves and I've requested you personally. Tomorrow morning. I'll be waiting. You can use a hammer and nails, can't you?" she asks.

"Not really," I confess.

Cook sighs heavily. "I'll build the shelves myself. Just what *have* you learned in America?"

Oh, there's a list a mile long: how to ride a motorcycle, the best way to eat a burrito, E is energy, m is mass, and c is the speed of light. But in the presence of my old nanny, my playmate, my storyteller, and my nurse, I am mute. I can remember nothing.

FORTY-THREE

CHILDHOOD LIVES ON IN THE BODY, long after we have grown too old for sledding or pasting red hearts onto purple paper. But we can return if we want to. Trace the elephantine bark of a cedar with the tips of your fingers. Dip your face into a pot of marigolds. If you do this, you will resurrect your smallest self.

I'm sitting in Cook's sun-soaked kitchen. She's made me flan and I've eaten nearly half the dish. I'm voraciously hungry. I swirl my fingers into the burnt sugar syrup and lick them like a savage.

"I'm not here to stay," I tell her. "My mother's dying. She's sent me to get her Seerskin and bring it back."

There are violet smudges under Cook's eyes. She hasn't slept well the entire time I've been in Isaura. Ever since she saw me outside the Ministry eating my lunch twelve days ago.

"She can't control her visions. She sees the future all the time. Without even touching people," I say.

"But she's got no Seerskin," says Cook. "She *can't* see the future anymore."

"Yes, she can," I tell her. "The magic works differently on Earth than it does here. Her visions came back. She can't stop them."

Cook shakes her head. "I told her," she says.

"Told her what?"

She ignores my question. "Why does she want her skin back? What good will that do?"

"We think the magic works in reverse on Earth. So if without her skin she can see the future . . ." I begin.

"Then with her skin, she won't see it anymore," finishes Cook.

"Yes," I say. "It'll stop the visions from coming."

Cook's mouth is pulled into a thin line. "You're going to give up that face?" she asks softly.

Cook always knew what I was feeling, even before I did.

"Do I look like him?" I ask.

"Who?" she says gently.

"My father," I say, exhaling quickly. To talk about him, to bring him into a conversation is to unwind the days. To make it as if he died yesterday.

Cook leans forward, astonished. "You can't tell?"

I shake my head. "It's hard for me to remember him. All I can think of is coming out into the kitchen, seeing him on the floor—" I break off.

Cook's face hardens. "No child should have to go through that," she says.

"My parents shouldn't have had to go through that," I remind her.

Cook's jaw saws back and forth. "No, you don't look like him."

I nod, oddly relieved.

"So Serena sent you back to get her Seerskin?" Cook asks a moment later. It's clear what she thinks of this.

"She had no choice: she's gone nearly crazy with the visions. She foresaw her own death," I say.

I defend my mother, but in this bright kitchen my voice sounds pathetic, as if it couldn't make a dent in the room's gleaming surface. Suddenly I feel ashamed for my mother and I'm not sure why. I stare down into the dish of custard.

Cook gets up abruptly and goes to the kitchen cupboard. The shelves are lined with canisters of herbs. "I'm going to make you a tea. You'll need to drink this every day. At least once. Twice is better," she says.

"Why?" I hate tea. Cook knows this.

"It'll stop the Change," she says.

"But I don't want to stop the Change," I say.

Cook looks at me steely eyed. "I'm not talking about your face. The *other* Change. The Change to your personality. Maybe it hasn't affected you yet. Maybe you haven't been here long enough," she says.

Oh, *that* Change. The confirmation feels almost anticlimactic. "Doesn't seem all that bad to me," I say. "Besides, I'm leaving in a few days." I fight to keep the misery from my voice.

"Just in case," Cook says, digging through the cupboard.

Just in case you stay is what she means. There has never been one moment in my entire life that Cook has not been on my side.

Cook sprinkles a mixture of herbs into a mug filled

with boiling water and brings it to the table. I take a cautious sip and groan; it tastes horrible.

"Never mind the taste—just drink it," says Cook.

I take a gulp and I'm overcome with guilt, as if by just taking one sip of the tea, I'm betraying my mother.

"I'm going to find her Seerskin and bring it back home," I pronounce.

Cook nods. "And where do you intend to find it?"

"It's somewhere in the Ministry."

"Perhaps," Cook says.

"No, it's got to be in the Ministry. I've been here fifteen days. I only have nine days left," I say.

Cook sighs. "How many days you have left doesn't matter."

We build the shelves for her pantry together. I hand her the nails, she pounds them in, and when we are done, I take a nap. I sleep in the same bed I slept in in the days following the fire. The sheets smell of lemon and I bury my nose in them, trying to remain a boy, but when I wake, it's dusk and I'm seventeen. I get up and stare at myself in the mirror. How is it that nothing of my father remains in my face?

FORTY-FOUR

I LEAVE COOK'S HOUSE AND my thoughts are pulled back to Phaidra. How did she spend the day? Did she eat ham for breakfast? Did she finish *Anna Karenina* yet? It's intolerable to think twelve hours have passed without my seeing her.

I think now of Phaidra's entire life. I imagine it spread out before me, the wide span of years that claim her as their own. She learned the alphabet, swam in rivers, and grew her hair long and I never knew she existed. What I don't let myself think about is her suffering. I only want to think of her as perfect and whole.

Nine days left with her, in this face. Do I tell her why I'm really here, who I really am? Or do I just live those days right to the end?

I've missed dinner. I hurry back to the house, hoping there will be some opportunity, some excuse to slip out tonight and meet Phaidra before I go to the Ministry to search for my mother's skin. Dash is sitting on the steps of the porch, waiting for me. I see the cherry red tip of his cigarette before I see him. He's taken a shower; his blond hair is damp. There are still lines left in it from the comb.

"How's it going?" he asks.

"Fine," I say perfunctorily, hoping to cut off the conversation.

"Phaidra's taught you to use something besides a broom?"

I ignore him. "Is there anything to eat?"

"Some bread. Cold chicken." He flicks his ashes on the ground. "Girls should be here soon. Who's coming tonight?"

Mee-Yon and Veronica. I forgot they were coming. "I'm exhausted," I say. "I'm going to bed. Can you tell them I'm sick?"

"I can, but I won't. Getting tired of all the attention?"

"Come on," I plead.

Dash stands and leans lazily against a pillar. He moves his body in a feral, predatory way.

"If you're real nice, I might fill in for you tonight," he says.

I let out a little snort of skepticism before I can stop it. Dash's face darkens, but the lazy smile remains.

"Have you ever been to Spain?" he asks.

He inhales, his eyes squinting, with pain or pleasure, I can't tell. Perhaps both—they aren't so different after all.

"The Mediterranean? The water has a funny taste. Metallic." He picks a speck of tobacco off his tongue delicately and wipes his finger on his pants. "I fell in love with a girl named Graciela."

Oh God. I'm famished. He's reaching out to me and I find myself annoyed. I've got neither the time nor the patience to develop a relationship with him. I think of the bread. I will eat the loaf whole.

"Are you in love, T?" he asks.

I shake my head.

He laughs. "Come on, you can tell me the truth."

"I'm telling you the truth," I say.

"Well, that's funny, because you're exhibiting all the signs of somebody who's in love. Which girl is it?"

"I'm hungry," I say.

Dash tosses his cigarette butt to the ground and stamps it out with the heel of his boot. "I know you're hungry, T," he says, in a voice just short of a snarl. "But you're going to have to learn to put your hunger aside."

Now I get it. He's talking about Phaidra.

"So, the book," he says, crossing his arms.

Damn, I knew his overlooking my Barker's was too good to be true. He's been waiting for just the right time to bring it up. Suddenly I remember that my name is written in the front of the primer. The scrawl of a five-year-old boy—and it says Thomas Gale, not Thomas Quicksilver. He must know Barker's is not some arbitrary book I swiped from the Ministry library.

"'Barker's Juvenile Primer No. 3: Containing pertinent moral and historical lessons for the edification and improvement of all Isaurian children,'" he quotes. "Where'd you get it, Quicksilver?"

I stare at him, my mouth agape. Even though I knew this moment might come, I am remarkably unprepared for it.

He cocks his head. "I guess the better question is *why*," he says. "Why do you have it?"

"I don't know," I tell him. And this is the truth. I don't know why I brought it with me. Certainly not for the map of the Ministry, whose layout is etched in my mind. It was the stupidest thing I could have done.

"Who are you?"

"Please don't ask," is all I can think to say.

"Who the hell are you?" Dash repeats, loudly.

"You know who I am," I whisper, pleading with him not to take this any further.

His eyes narrow.

"Right. You're the asshole who thinks everybody's always looking at him," he says. He grabs his sweater, which is draped over the porch railing. "You leave her alone, you hear me?" He stalks off in the direction of the

Refectory. "Don't let me hear you've disappointed those girls," he calls out.

"Where are you going?" I say, trying to gauge just exactly how much trouble I'm in.

"Java time," he says.

Relief floods through me. He's not turning me in—not yet, anyway.

He turns around. "Want me to bring you back one?"

"Um, sure."

"Um, keep dreaming," he says.

FORTY-FIVE

SCREW THE CONNECTICUTS. DASH KNOWS something's up and I've got an hour tops before he comes home. I find Phaidra in the common room of her dorm. It's a place where they store all the junk. There's a shabby, stained couch. Run-down upholstered chairs with the stuffing bursting out of the seams. Phaidra sits on the floor, her back to the wall. I stand in the doorway, panting.

"You weren't at supper," she says.

"I've brought you something." I hand her the little packet of herbs Cook gave me. "You can stop cutting yourself now. Crush these and make a tea out of it. You need to drink it every day."

She opens the package and sniffs. She makes a face. "What is this stuff?"

"It'll slow down the process. The leaking," I tell her.

She slides up the wall to her feet, alarmed. "Who gave you this?"

"There are things I have to tell you."

"Clearly," she says.

The room is empty except for us. There aren't any lamps, but there is a window, and the night streams in, bathing us in a violet light.

"My name is Thomas Gale," I begin.

FORTY-SIX

WE'RE SILENT, WALKING BACK ACROSS the green. She hasn't said a word to me since I've told her everything. Who I am. Why I'm here. What I must do.

"Say something. Say anything," I plead.

"What's there to say? You're leaving in nine days."

I grab her arm. "Come with me. You know you hate it here."

She shakes me off angrily. "That's not possible."

"Why not? I don't care what was wrong with you."

"I do," she says icily.

"Well, I don't." But even as I say it, I'm not sure I believe it. The thought of going back home with my old burned face is unbearable, never mind having to deal with adjusting to Phaidra's affliction. But I want to try. I do. I want to believe this has made me stronger.

"Oh, Thomas." She whirls around to face me. "You're a dreamer, aren't you?"

"No, I'm not," I shout. "Goddamn it, Phaidra!"

"God's not here," she says harshly. "God's never been anywhere near me."

I grab her arm and pull her close.

"That isn't true," I say. I cup her ears with my hands and shake her head gently. "God's here." I touch my fingers to her lips. "And here." I stroke her cheek.

She tosses her head miserably. "What if you stayed?" she asks.

"I can't."

"But what if you did? We could drink Cook's tea. Maybe it would stop the leaking for good. We could . . . we could just live here."

We could play house. She could fix holes in the roof with her hammer and I'd sweep up after.

"If I stay, my mother will die," I say.

Her head bobs frantically; she's searching for an answer. There isn't one. A little sound of panic escapes her.

"I didn't count on meeting you," I say.

"Then you have to go. I won't throw myself in front of a train, if that's what you're worried about," she says.

She begins to cry. She doesn't cry like a normal girl. The tears spring out of her eyes, but her face doesn't crinkle up at all.

"We'll find a way," I tell her, desperate to convince both her and myself. "Alice wants to help us. Remember? We're not alone. We have Cook *and* the Maker."

Here it is, hope. I've managed to pull it out of my hat. It comes bop-bop-bopping along like a little rabbit on velvet paws

Phaidra is less convinced. She just looks at me forlornly.

"We'll figure it out," I tell her. "Trust me. You'll see."

FORTY-SEVEN

THE NEXT MORNING AT WORK, Otak makes a surprise visit.

"When will you be done?" he asks Brian.

"Two weeks," says Brian calmly. He's approaching seven hundred days. I don't think he'd make a fuss if I knocked him unconscious with my broom.

"One week," says Otak.

"All right," Brian agrees.

Phaidra and I are staining a cabinet. We keep our eyes pasted to our work.

"You two!" Otak yells.

I turn around slowly, with dread.

"Yes, you. And the girl," says Otak. "A bird flew into my window again. This time it's broken. I want it fixed by this afternoon."

With a flurry of his robes Otak disappears, a cadre of Seers trailing after him.

Phaidra glances at me. Her eyebrows do a little victory dance at our good fortune. My heart presses painfully against my rib cage, trapped. *Not yet*. I don't want to go yet.

I pick up my brush and dip it into the stain. Slowly I run the bristles down the length of the cabinet.

"Quicksilver?" says Phaidra. "Did you hear him?"

I nod. "We should finish this," I say.

Phaidra takes the brush out of my hand. "Someone else will finish."

•   •   •

I halfheartedly search while Phaidra fixes the window. I make a show of pawing through Otak's drawers and wardrobe. I open the boxes in the back of his closet. I press the tiles of the fireplace, looking for secret doors. Panic overtakes me as I finally admit to myself the truth. I don't want to find my mother's Seerskin.

"She told me it would be here," I say dismally, trying to cover up my ambivalence.

Phaidra's caulking the new window. "Did you honestly think you'd find it stuffed in his drawer?" she says. "Think outside the box."

"I hate that expression," I say.

"Well, it applies here," she says.

"Damn!"

Phaidra looks at me calmly. "You're going about this all wrong."

"What if he shredded it up into tiny pieces?" I ask.

"I'm sure he didn't do that," she says. "It's here. *Somewhere.*"

I groan. She's such a better person than I am.

"It could be anywhere in Isaura!" I say.

I think of the bird, the second one that crashed into Otak's window. Was it the offspring of the first bird that had died? Was it so filled with sorrow, so overwhelmed with grief it decided to follow its mother into death?

"I don't want to go back, Phaidra," I say.

Phaidra climbs down off the windowsill. She pulls a rag from her back pocket and wipes her scraper clean of the caulking. She's thinking, carefully composing her response, but I can't stand that she's not answering me immediately. I want her to absolve me for saying such a blasphemous thing, but I can't help what my heart wants—to stay with her in Isaura, where we're both beautiful and whole. I take the scraper out of her hand and hurl it across the room. "What if it's her time to die?" I shout.

Suddenly I feel claustrophobic. I run to the window and open it. I stick my head out and look down at the ground, gulping in huge breaths of air. I don't know what I'm expecting to find. The remains of the bird are gone, but I can see the ghost of it splayed out on the cobblestones: its bones of straw, a wing wrapped around its tiny head. If I held it in my hand, would it smell of sky?

"You can't give up," says Phaidra softly.

"Give up on what?" asks Otak.

"Give up on carpentry," says Phaidra, without missing a beat. She turns around and smiles patronizingly at me. "He's no natural, but I keep telling him practice makes—"

"For a dull life indeed," finishes Otak. "If you're practicing something you have no aptitude for." He walks to the window and runs his finger across the glass.

"Nicely done." He turns to me. "You should think about finding yourself a new vocation. Now, shall I ring Roberta for some tea?" he asks pleasantly.

"No," I say. I can't stand the charade any longer. Underneath that charming exterior is a monster.

"Thomas needs to get back early today," Phaidra says.

"Go," says Otak, dismissing me. "You'll stay," he says to Phaidra. It's a command, not a question.

"It's all right if I'm late," I say quickly, not wanting to leave her alone with him.

"Very well, then," says Otak.

Roberta raps at the door and walks into the room.

"Tea for three," Otak tells her.

We spend the rest of the afternoon with him. He interviews us on all things that have to do with America. He's like Jane Goodall conducting a study on the gorillas and when we leave, I feel robbed, like my pockets have been picked while I was bending down to tie my shoe.

FORTY-EIGHT

WHEN I TELL DASH THAT I'm done with the Connecticuts, he says no way.

"No way what?" I ask.

"No way will I allow it."

We're stacking wood. Well, I'm stacking wood—he's splitting it; I'm not to be trusted with an ax. The backyard is punctuated by his grunts as the blade pivots through the air. He's an efficiency machine. Not one iota of energy is wasted. Secretly I've been studying his moves.

"Why would you even care?" I ask, but I know the answer. He thinks if I'm seeing the Connecticuts, he won't have to worry about me with Phaidra.

"They're boring," I add.

He wipes the sweat off his forehead with a bandana. "Life is boring. You just put up with it."

"I'm done putting up with things," I say.

Dash slams the ax down into the chopping block in one graceful arc. Wood chips fly everywhere, including my left eye. I rub my eye vigorously and jump around on one foot. He looks at me with disgust; once again I'm overreacting.

"I'm with Phaidra," I say angrily. "That's why I broke it off with the others."

Dash shakes his head. "'Fraid not, kid."

"Look, I don't know what went on between the two of you," I say. "And to be honest, I don't really want to know. But we're together now."

"That so?"

"Yeah," I say.

Dash tosses a piece of wood over his shoulder and it lands neatly on the pile.

"There's the little matter of the book," he says.

"You tell them whatever you want to about the book. I stole it from the Ministry. It was a bad call. I'll apologize; I'll accept my punishment and move on," I say.

"No," says Dash. "That's not how it's going down. Don't think I'm not on to you. You're going to hurt her. I don't know how or why, but you're going to break her heart. And I won't let you," he says, his finger stabbing the air in front of me.

"You don't have any say in it," I retort. "Things haven't gone your way. You lost. You didn't get Phaidra. I did. Now get over it."

My vision has cleared up, unfortunately. Just in time to see him toggle the ax out of the chopping block, grab it with one meaty hand, and lumber toward me. I look around frantically for help . . . and see Emma.

"Put that down," she cries.

Dash grabs me around the neck and throws me up against the woodpile. I can hear Patrick's voice in my head running down a list of potential countermoves from wrestling: the Corkcrew Moonsault, the Gorry Special, and the Samoan Drop. No, no, and no. I reject them all (might have something to do with the fact that I can remember none of the moves, only their names). What's needed is something simple. Just as I'm about to ram my knee up into Dash's groin, he hefts the ax, spins the head around, and slices my cheek with the razor-sharp edge of the gleaming blade.

"Think you're such a prize," he hisses.

"No, that would be you," I say, blood seeping out from between my fingers.

Meanwhile Emma's got her hands around his waist and is trying to peel him off me. "Get away from Thomas!" she cries.

"Don't fall in love with her!" he roars.

"Is that an ultimatum?"

"Consider it a warning."

"Well, it's too late," I yell at him.

"Dash!" I hear a woman's voice. It's Nancy, the Head Host.

This time Dash listens. He backs away from me slowly. Even unflappable Nancy is taken aback when she sees the blood streaming down my face.

"What happened?" she asks.

Emma's trying to mop up the blood with the sleeve of her shirt. I take her hand away. She nods, but I can see she's terribly upset. I draw her into my hip protectively.

"He just went crazy," I say to Nancy.

Dash doesn't say a word in his defense and this astounds me. Now would be the perfect time to turn me in. Instead he just looks at me tiredly and somehow I feel like I'm the one who's betrayed him.

"Dash—you're on probation as of now," says Nancy. "Thomas 16 will be transferred to my house immediately."

"No," says Dash. "Give me one more week to prove myself."

"You've just sliced open his cheek," says Nancy.

"It was a little scratch," he says.

The blood is copious, but I realize he's right. This is a little scratch compared to everything else I've been through in my life. I stand there, panting, trying to make sense of what's just happened. As my heart races and I try and catch my breath, I realize it felt good; I've never been in a position to fight over a girl before. And then I know why Dash hasn't turned me in. There is a code of honor between us. You can cut each other open. But you will not give each other up.

"I'll stay," I tell her.

"What?" asks Nancy, swiveling around.

I shrug. "I was asking for it."

She eyes me distrustfully. "Well, since you seem to

be so suddenly fond of each other, one week. After that you move to my house." She takes the ax out of Dash's hands and props it up against the woodpile. "You, meet me in the Refectory in ten minutes."

Dash walks away. Nancy takes my chin in her hand and turns my face to the left. "You better get to the infirmary. They'll have some sort of salve to aid the healing."

"I'll take him," chirps Emma.

Nancy looks down at Emma like she's a shrub she's just stumbled over. "You do that, little girl." Then she looks back at me. "You have quite the fan club."

"No, ma'am," I say.

"I'll be watching you, Thomas."

And she does. She watches Emma and me until we disappear from her sight. And even after we have entered the infirmary, she is still watching, standing by the woodpile, her hand resting lightly on the ax.

FORTY-NINE

It's after midnight when Dash returns. I've fallen asleep at the table. He kicks the leg of my chair, waking me. "Get to bed."

"What happened?" I mumble, my speech slurred with sleep.

"What the hell do you think happened?"

"You're in trouble?"

He sneers. "I'm on probation. You think that's a good thing?"

"Look, I'm sorry," I begin.

"Stow it."

He rummages through the back of a cabinet and pulls out a bottle of whiskey. He pours himself two fingers' worth, sits down, and tosses the amber liquid down his throat.

"I'll stay here," I say. "I won't go to Nancy's."

"Too late for that."

"Well, maybe it's for the best. That way you won't have to see me and . . ."

He glares at me and pours himself another shot.

"Can I have some?" I ask.

He looks at me disdainfully. "You're pathetic, Quicksilver."

"Maybe," I say. "Probably."

He empties the glass and then rolls it across the table with his palm. "Imagine this is you. You're in the middle of a lake. Sitting in a rowboat. One oar in the water," he says.

"What is this?" I blurt. "A sample question from the SATs?"

Dash glares at me. "Just shut up and listen for once."
He runs his finger around the lip of his glass. "Here you
are. Spinning around in circles."

"Just get to the point."

"Let me ask you something, Thomas."

"What, already?" I say.

The last thing my father said to me was, *I'll be here
when you get back.* A lie, of course, for he was about to
die. He would never be back. But what's the fuss? It's
only one lie out of the millions to be filed with all the rest
of the lies that children are told. But a lie such as this has
a blunt tip and it slowly works its way into the body, week
by week, year by year. Until one day you find you have
been tunneled. Within you is a trench through which the
twin currents of grief and betrayal flow.

Dash lunges forward. "When are you going to put
both damn oars in the water and row?"

FIFTY

Cook summons me. This time it's under the aus-
pices of repairing the roof of her garden shed. It's a
bright, cool morning. When I arrive, she's waiting in

the front yard. She wades though her garden to greet me. The door of her house is flung wide open and it gapes at me like an angry mouth. Something's not right. She hands me two things: a letter and a butcher's knife.

"These belong to you. I should have given them to you long ago. I'm sorry, Thomas," she says.

The letter is from my father and the knife—well, the last time I saw it was the day he died. Horrified, I let it drop to the ground.

Slowly, with trembling hands, I unfold the letter.

This morning your mother made waffles. You sat at the table, humming. You ate like a bear cub, stabbing the pieces with your fork and catapulting them into your mouth. I can barely stand to look at you. Your goodness dazzles me. The perfection of an eight-year-old boy.

Of all I have done and accomplished, I am most proud of you.

Here is the answer to your question. There is no seam. You must slice the skin open and then peel it off. Your mother and I believe in what we are doing. We will shed our skins as easily as stepping out of a pair of pants and then we will be free of this curse. Believe me, even if it turns out I am telling you lies.

Here is my wish for you. It is not so very different from what all fathers wish for their sons:

May you swim in warm seas.

May you never go to war.

May you one day forgive us.

I read the letter a second time and then a third, trying to absorb it. Finally I let it flutter to the ground. The Ministry didn't flay my parents of their Seerskins. They did it to themselves.

Noises that aren't human come out of my mouth. A string of gurgles and gasps.

"Thomas," Cook says. "Breathe."

She reaches out to touch me and I bat her away.

"I wanted to tell you," she explains. "Your mother wouldn't let me. She said she'd tell you when the time was right. Come inside. I'll make tea." She glances nervously at the neighbors' house.

"Screw your tea," I say coldly.

Cook grabs my elbow. "They did it because they wanted a better life for you. They wanted to leave Isaura, Thomas."

"We *had* to leave. Otak banished us!" I cry.

"No, he didn't," says Cook. "Your mother traded her skin for passage to Earth. That was the plan all along. To barter with her skin to get out."

I stare at Cook in silence. Suddenly she looks a hundred years old. She was young once. This woman who used to make me corn muffins, who cut my fingernails—who has lied to me just like everybody else.

"You can't go back in this state," says Cook. "You've got to calm down."

"You're right," I tell her.

"Good," says Cook, clearly relieved I've come to my senses.

"I'm not going back," I say. It's clear to both of us that I'm not talking about the Compound.

Her face crumples.

"All these years my mother has let me believe she's the victim. *I* was burned. *I'm* the victim," I tell her.

"You were all victims," says Cook.

"You want to know what they call me at school? *Pucker,*" I hiss.

"I'm sorry, Thomas," Cook says gently. "I'm so terribly sorry."

"It doesn't matter anymore. None of it matters. I've got a second chance. I'm not going back to Earth."

"But she was doing what she thought was best for you," Cook persists.

"Really?" I ask. "Lying to me all these years? Sending me back here?"

"Thomas, don't. You're better than this," Cook exclaims.

"I'm not better than this. I've tried to be better, but I'm not."

"I never should have given you that letter." Cook reaches up to touch my cheek. "I did this to you."

"Yes, you did," I say, brushing her hand away. "You all did."

FIFTY-ONE

I LEAVE COOK'S HOUSE CLUTCHING another bag of the tea that will stop the Change. Cook doesn't realize that showing me that letter was a favor. She's set me free by telling me the truth.

That evening I gather my group together. We meet down by the river; I don't want to risk being seen. As I explain to them about the Change and what it does to our personalities, I empty the tea out onto a cloth on the ground. I half expect a round of applause. I have, after all, just revealed myself as their savior. Certainty fills me with its white light. I feel hard, brilliant, empty.

"What's she doing here?" Michael says, glaring at Phaidra, who stands beside me. "She's not in our group."

"She is now," I say.

I sift through the pile of tea, tossing out twigs and an errant blossom. Michael is predictably unimpressed.

"Tea?" He picks up a handful and sniffs it. His face wrinkles in disgust and he crushes the herbs before dropping them on the ground. "Smells like marijuana."

"Smells like you're an idiot," I say. "Don't waste it."

"I'm not drinking that crap," Michael replies.

"Fine," I say. "Come see me in a hundred days when you've turned into Mr. Roboto."

"I'll drink it," says Emma.

"We're all drinking it," I say. "Twice a day. Morning and night." I divide the mound of tea into six portions.

"We'll get into trouble," Rose moans, wringing her hands.

"It's worth the risk," I say. "Nobody has to know. Just be careful."

"So what's the deal with this cook?" Michael asks.

I haven't told them everything. Only that there are Isaurians who want to help us and that I had the good fortune of working for one—a cook who gave me the tea.

"It doesn't matter. She's just somebody who feels bad for us."

"Why?" asks Michael suspiciously, eyeing the diminishing pile of herbs.

I sigh. "Look. If you're not interested in saving yourself, then go away."

"I *am* saved!" Michael shouts. "And you want me to screw it up."

"I'm trying to help you," I say.

"Who in God's name asked for your help?"

Phaidra puts her hand on my forearm to stop me from speaking. "Nobody's trying to trick you," she says softly to Michael.

"Fine, then I want my share," Michael says petulantly.

"Here. Take mine. I'll get more." I throw my portion into a bag and hand it to him.

"I'm not saying I'll drink it," he replies.

I shake my head. "Will you just take it and stop

being so suspicious? It's tea. You obviously didn't have a problem eating or drinking whatever was put in front of you before."

The group falls silent at my words. I feel a twinge of shame, but it's distant, impersonal. Nothing can touch me right now.

Michael stares at me hard. When he finally speaks, he mumbles quietly, "You shouldn't have said that." He slams the bag of tea into my chest.

"He didn't mean it," Phaidra interjects.

"Yes, he did," Michael replies, and then he gets up and leaves.

FIFTY-TWO

That night Phaidra comes for me.

She doesn't stand in the backyard and toss pebbles at my window. Instead she comes in through the front door. She pads noiselessly to my room and taps me on the shoulder. The scent of roses rises from her just-washed hair.

"What is it?" I ask.

"Shhh," she says, pulling me out of bed.

We tiptoe down the hall. Dash's snores fill the house. She clamps her hand over her mouth so she won't giggle. Once we get outside, we run. Her nightgown glows blue in the moonlight, like a hard-boiled egg. She takes me down to the river.

"Wait up," I shout.

She wades into the water. "No more waiting," she calls out.

There is a boy. There is a girl. There is some invisible tether that connects them. I follow her into the river. Her nightgown floats up around her like a halo.

"Now, under," she says.

I take her hand and we dive deep into the water, down to the bottom. We grab handfuls of cattails before the current takes us. When we cannot hold our breath any longer; we surface and swim with long, clean strokes to the river's edge.

"Your nightgown," I whisper. It's plastered to her body. I can see every curve, every notch, every groove of her. I try not to stare, but it's impossible.

She pulls it up over her head and tosses it on the ground beside her.

When I touch her, she shudders. But we are not alone. All that we were pulses beside us.

"Ghosts," I say. "Get out."

I take her head in my hands and smooth the hair back from her temples.

I kiss her forehead, her damp cheeks; I kiss the thumbprint indentation above her upper lip.

"My eyes," she whispers. "You've forgotten my eyes."

She closes her eyes and I kiss the lids. My lips come away wet.

"I never was with Dash. He wants everyone to think I was, but it never happened," she says.

Oh, my girl. My stubborn, clear-hearted girl.

"I'm going to stay, Phaidra. I've figured out a way," I tell her.

Her face floods with happiness and then worry. "But Thomas . . . your mother—"

I put my hand over her mouth, silencing her. Then I lean her back gently into the river grass.

FIFTY-THREE

WHEN I WAKE THE NEXT MORNING, I'm light-headed from lack of sleep. Phaidra left a few hours ago. I still feel some layer of her pressed up against me, as if she's forgotten to take her shadow along with her.

I go back to the Compound. It's deserted. The scent of bread unfurls from the Refectory, but there's still an hour until breakfast. I haven't given a thought to my mother; my mind is completely filled with Phaidra, with the hours that we spent together.

Still, a finger of guilt worms its way in at the edges of my consciousness. I feel horrible for how I left things with Cook. If I'm to stay in Isaura, I've got to go work it out with her.

I walk beside myself this morning, as if there are two of me. I gasp when I replay last night in my head. I slow my stride when I reach Cook's gate.

"Phaidra." I say her name once to calm me.

"Oh, Phaidra," I say again.

Cook's house has been burned to the ground.

FIFTY-FOUR

I SPRINT TO THE NEIGHBORS' and ring the bell. It takes a long time for anyone to answer. Finally a woman opens the door.

"You did it. You set Adalia's house on fire," she says simply.

"What?" I cry.

"Well, you might as well have," she says. "The Ministry knows all about you now, *Thomas Gale*."

When I hear my true name spoken out loud in Isaura, everything drops away. It's all over now. I stare at her in a stunned silence.

The woman glares at me. "Don't you want to know about Adalia?" she asks.

Oh God, Cook. "Was she hurt?" I burst out.

The woman shrugs. "That remains to be seen," she says, and then shuts the door.

"No, wait!" I run to the window and rap on the glass. "Please!" I yell.

Panic blooms in my mouth, a red flower with a thousand petals.

"You're the one they're looking for," a voice says behind me.

I whirl around. A small boy watches me solemnly.

"You better go. She'll tell them you've come back," he says in an eerily adult voice. He can't be more than five years old.

"Who burned her house down?" I ask, although I know it was the Ministry.

He shrugs.

"Where is she?"

"They took her."

"Jesus," I bleat. They are going to make an example of her. Punishment for helping me.

The boy looks at me calmly. "What do you want?" he asks.

"What I can't have," I whisper.

I spend the day hiding in the woods. When night falls, I creep back to the Compound. I peek in the Refectory windows: dinner is long over; the kitchen staff is hard at work washing dishes and wiping down the long tables. I glance across the green; Dash's house is dark. This is not a good sign. I squat in the bushes.

I'm not there for long before Rose and Emma come walking down the path holding hands. They're talking softly. I grab Emma's arm and yank her down next to me. She gives a small shriek and I clamp my hand over her mouth. "It's me," I whisper. Slowly Rose lowers her hand to her chest.

"My God, you gave me a fright," she says.

Emma relaxes in my arms. "I'm sorry, kid," I tell her. She stares up at me beatifically; then her face prunes up with worry.

"Where have you been?" she asks. "Everyone's looking for you." She strokes the back of my hand. It's a disturbingly maternal gesture, coming from an eleven-year-old girl.

Rose joins us in the bushes. Tiny diamonds of light from the mullioned Refectory windows spill down on us. For the first time since this morning I feel safe; then I think of Cook.

"They burned her house down," I say.

"Whose house?" asks Rose.

"Cook. The woman who gave us the tea."

Rose inhales sharply.

"That jerk!" Emma cries. "It's his fault."

"Who's fault?" I ask.

"Michael. He did it—I'm sure of it. He told Dash that you gave us the tea. He probably told them about Cook, too."

"You should have treated him with more respect," admonishes Rose. "You should have been kinder. He's suffered as much as the rest of us."

"I know," I say.

"And you're sorry?" Rose asks, expecting compassion.

I nod. I *am* sorry. Because of Michael my life is over.

FIFTY-FIVE

W HEN I GET TO THE MINISTRY, it's deserted. No guards. Nobody patrolling the grounds. I walk right through the front door.

"Thomas," Phaidra says as I step into the Maker's room.

I'm startled to see her—and confused. "What are you doing here?" I ask.

She's sitting in a chair. Her hair is pulled back with a blue velvet ribbon. Tendrils swoop down her long, elegant neck like streamers.

"Waiting for you," she says.

Her answer makes no sense, but neither does anything else anymore. "Everything's fallen apart," I tell her. "They know who I am. They've taken Cook."

Phaidra moans softly, but she doesn't move from her chair.

"Phaidra, come on, let's go. We've got to find Cook."

She stands, extends her hand to me. "I don't know if I'll be much help," she says.

"What are you talking about?" I say, grabbing her hand and pulling. She stumbles.

"Wait, not so quickly," she says. "Please." Her voice is miniature.

"Phaidra, we have to hurry," I say, pulling again. She nearly falls, but I catch her and with a small cry she frantically touches my face, my eyes, my nose.

I swat at her, irritated that she's playing games. "Did you hear me?"

"They Changed me back, Thomas," she says dully.

"What? There's nothing wrong with you. You're perfect."

I let go of her suddenly and her hands paw wildly at the air. Then I see what's different. The girl whose gaze was creek-cold and clear as a November night—her gaze is now blank.

"I'm blind," she says. "I've been blind since I was six years old. That's why I came to Isaura." She laughs softly. "Funny thing, though. It's not so bad to be changed back. You won't believe it. It's almost a relief."

I stare at her in disbelief.

"I came looking for your mother's Seerskin and I was caught," Phaidra confesses. "That's why they Changed me back."

Her pupils are freakishly large. Like saucers.

"No," I say. "Tell me you didn't do that."

"I was trying to help," she says softly.

"I didn't ask for your help," I whisper.

"I had to. You'd given up. I couldn't let your mother die," she cries.

If only she could see me. See how my movie star face falls in on itself now, like a cake that is missing its eggs.

"I knew you would change your mind. You would have regretted giving up," she says desperately.

But she's wrong. Like everybody else, she thinks far too much of me.

I take a step backward. "I have to find Cook," I whisper.

"Take me with you," she insists. "I want to go back with you. I don't care about being blind. I don't care about your face. I won't even be able to see you."

"Well, how fortunate for you," I say.

"That's not what I mean!" she exclaims. Her eyes dart frantically to the left and right. "God, I can't believe you're acting this way."

Below the fringe of her lashes, two blue pendulums.

"Thomas, please," she begs.

Everybody I love has betrayed me: my mother, my father, Cook, and now Phaidra.

"You're going to leave me, aren't you?" she says.

When I don't answer, she laughs. "What a shame. We would have been a perfect match on Earth. Quasimodo and Helen Keller."

I tiptoe backward. She's an anchor wrapped

around my waist. And I have far too many anchors already.

"I can hear you leaving," she shouts. "I'm not deaf!"

But she doesn't see me leave.

FIFTY-SIX

How quickly we make the ones we love into *other*.

I leave the Ministry and stumble down to the river. I go to a cave that Phaidra once showed me. A place where she had hidden away to read her forbidden books. I want to hibernate.

Against the back wall I find a mattress fashioned out of grass and next to it a stack of Phaidra's stolen books: *Ulysses, My Antonia, One Flew Over the Cuckoo's Nest.* Now I understand why she read so voraciously. She had been blind. She was making up for lost time.

I open *My Antonia* and drape it across my chest like a flag. The smell of the book comforts me. It's the scent of my childhood: a time when I believed stories could save your life. I think of my mother. Is she even conscious anymore? Is she is in terrible pain? I've failed her. I've failed everybody who's had the misfortune to depend on me.

"Thomas, get up." Someone shakes my shoulder. I must have fallen asleep. I jerk upright and haul the book over my head in an attack position.

"Put that book down," says Rose.

I lower it slowly. She hands me a sandwich. It's tomato and cheese. The bread is all soggy, but I don't care—I gobble it up. Food has never tasted so good.

"Phaidra's missing," Rose says.

I nod.

"Did you hear me?"

"I heard you."

"And?" She places her hands on her hips.

"She's not missing."

Rose raises her eyebrows.

"She's at the Ministry. They Changed her back," I say.

"My God, why?" Rose asks, her face flushed with shock. She looks at me sprawled on the grass, the books scattered about me. "And why are you lying around like you're on vacation?"

"You don't understand," I say lifelessly. "There are

things I haven't told you. Things that make this complicated."

"Why don't you make me understand, then," says Rose, glaring at me.

So I tell her—everything. It's not easy. I feel like a wrestler, pinned to the mat by my own despair, hopelessness, and shame, but somehow I manage to get the story out. When I'm done, Rose sinks down on the cave floor next to me.

"So they Changed Phaidra back because she was trying to help you. And you left her there." Rose looks anxiously at the entrance to the cave. "When are you going back to the Ministry?"

"Who said I was going back?"

Rose's mouth sags open. "You're just going to leave her there?"

Phaidra's face, her dead eyes, flash into my mind and I squeeze my eyes shut against the image. "She's better off without me."

"You mean you're better off without her."

"No!" I cry.

Rose leans forward angrily. "I have to go now. But you should know—you were the most stunning young man the first time I saw you—*before* you got Changed."

•   •   •

A while later I stick my head out of the cave and try and gauge what time it is by how high the sun is in the sky, but I'm miserable at that sort of thing. Phaidra would know; Phaidra could probably make a sundial out of twigs and a pile of deer droppings.

I'm strangely disoriented. The stitches holding the day in place have loosened and the hours are sliding about, colliding into one another. I crawl back onto the grass mattress. I try to read, but Willa's words won't stay in sentences, so I suck on the solitary images like cough drops: *brown pools, baked earth, copper-red grass.* In this way I give myself solace; I begin to patch myself together.

What a strange life this is, how vast and unfathomable. Some people believe a man can be molded from dust. I drift away once again, the bottomless sleep of the fucked.

"Wake up," whispers Emma. "Wake up." She's crawled onto the mattress and tucked herself under my arm.

I rise up on one elbow. "How long have you been here?"

"Just a few minutes," she says, plucking at my sleeve. "Rose told me what happened."

"Jesus," I mutter.

Emma looks at me indignantly. "I'm the one who loves you. She had to tell me."

I stare at Emma. The ends of her long brown curls are wet from where she's sucked on them.

"That's a bad habit," I say, picking up a lock of hair. "Didn't your mother ever tell you that?"

"Did you hear me?" she asks.

"I heard you."

"That I love you?"

"Emma," I say. "I'm not worth your time."

"You're the stupidest boy I ever met," she says. "Why don't you stop feeling sorry for yourself? It's boring." She sits up. "I don't love you that way, you know. The way Phaidra loves you."

"I know," I say.

"Good."

Something cracks in my chest. I can't believe this girl—her grace.

We sit in silence for a while. "Hey, Emma, do you have that picture? The one of your parents sitting in the rowboat?"

She looks at me suspiciously. "Why?"

"I wanted to see it again. I think I made a mistake," I say.

She rolls her eyes. "You didn't make a mistake. There was no space on the seat in the rowboat. My parents weren't thinking of me when they were out on the lake. They were escaping from me, from my life in the dark."

"You knew that?"

"Yes. I just needed to not believe it for a while. And guess what? I don't need to believe it anymore. My parents did their best with what they got."

A lesson. She is teaching me a lesson. This eleven-year-old, sunlight-deprived girl.

"The tea," I say. "Promise me you'll keep drinking the tea. And give it to the others so they'll stay whole."

I think of that first day when we all arrived: Jerome and Jesse shuffling along, attached at the chest; Rose and her Pacesaver Scout wheelchair; Emma and her protective clothing; Michael, his pockets stuffed with Twinkies and Ring Dings; and me, of course, Pucker. It seems like a lifetime ago, but I find myself filled with tenderness for the people that we were.

"You want me to give it to everybody?" asks Emma. "Not just our group?"

"Yes, everybody," I say, thinking of the Connecticuts and Brian.

"It'll be like a giant tea party. Like the Boston Tea Party!"

"They threw the tea overboard in Boston, Emma."

She grins. "I was making a joke."

We sit in a contented silence for a few minutes and I know it's the last bit of peace I'll have for a while.

I pray Phaidra will forgive me.

FIFTY-SEVEN

I'M SO LOST IN MY THOUGHTS, so intent on running as fast as I can to the Ministry, that I don't hear the sound of the wagon. The rig creaks to a halt and Dash glares down at me. "Get in, idiot," he says.

It doesn't occur to me to disobey him. I climb up and sit beside him, panting. He looks straight ahead, the reins wound tight around his knuckles.

"So—you got a plan?" he asks.

I shake my head, wondering what he's up to.

"You better have a plan," he says.

"What do you care?" I say. "You turned me in."

He snorts. "I didn't turn you in. You always think everyone's after you. Life isn't that black and white."

"Right," I say, running a hand through my hair, which is wet with sweat.

"That's not to say you're not in deep trouble," he adds.

"Thanks for the news flash."

He looks disgusted. "Could you for one minute stop being such a smartass? Are you capable of that?"

"Sorry," I say.

Dash lets his breath out loudly.

I run my hands down my thighs, pressing my fingers into the bones, hard. Everything aches. Anxiety has ironed my body flat.

"They Changed her back," I say. I can't bring myself to say Phaidra's name out loud.

Dash scowls. "Why do you think I'm here? I told you not to drag her into this. But you did anyway, you little shit."

He's right. I am a shit. We ride in silence for a few minutes.

"I didn't turn you in," Dash says finally. "I played dumb. But they put it together without me. They found your Barker's—it wasn't too hard."

"Why didn't you tell on me?" I can't stop myself from pushing, goading. "They probably would have given you an extra case of whiskey. Another carton of cigarettes."

Dash looks off into the distance, his jaw tight. "Because I saw you before you were Changed."

"So you helped me because you pitied me."

"No," Dash says, weariness in his voice. "I did it because I saw who you really were."

Gratitude wells up inside me, a hot sweetness that makes my throat throb. Everything comes too late, I think. What's important rings the bell just as you're putting on your coat and getting ready to walk out the door.

We drive around a bend and the city comes into sight. Dash stops the wagon.

"End of the line," he says.

I stare at him stupidly, not wanting to move.

He punches me lightly on the shoulder. "Out."

I climb down and stand there like a child, looking up at him.

"I don't have a plan," I say, suddenly bereft at the thought of him going.

"Both oars, T," says Dash steadily, looking me in the eyes. "Put both oars in the water and row."

FIFTY-EIGHT

THE TRUTH HAS LAYERS AND SO DO LIES.

At the last minute I change my mind about going to the Ministry. I'm following a hunch. I need to go home.

People stare at me and whisper as I walk down the

city streets. It seems my real identity is common knowledge now.

"So you've returned," Otak says when I walk into the yard of the house I grew up in. There is nothing left but a stone foundation. He's sitting on a tree stump, waiting for me. For some reason, this doesn't surprise me.

"Where's Cook?" I say.

"She's not in any danger," he says.

"You burned her house down!" I yell.

"*She* burned her house down," says Otak. "We may be many things, but we are not savages."

"You're lying," I say, my discomfort mounting.

"She said it didn't feel like home anymore," says Otak calmly.

I glare at him while I try and digest this information. Much to my annoyance, it sounds disturbingly like something Cook would say.

"Well, what about Phaidra? You had the Maker Change her back."

Otak nods. "She has not acclimated well," he says. "We simply accelerated the process of bringing her back to herself. Sometimes that happens. The Change is not a fit. Rarely, but it's not unheard of."

He studies me for a reaction. I squint off into the distance, my lips narrowed with rage. He has done this to me every time, with our every encounter. He turns the conversation. He turns *me*.

"I should have recognized you," he says. "You look just like your father."

"You're lying," I say loudly, but my retort is half-hearted, and we both know it.

"It's time someone told you the truth," he says.

Despite the fact that I want—no, I *need*—him to be a villain, my heart surges. This is the High Seer of Isaura, and when he says there is something of my father in me, it must be so.

I think of Cook. *She* must have lied to me. But as I said, there are layers to the truth, to lies as well, and perhaps this is part of the reason why I've traveled all this way—to find this out. Cook told me I looked nothing like my father because she wanted to protect me. She knew I was planning on going back to Earth, and that meant going back to being Pucker. Whether my unscarred face bore any resemblance to my father would soon be irrelevant.

And then Otak says something entirely unexpected from somebody who is my mortal enemy.

What he says is, "Stay."

Does he mean stay so that he can call the guards? Stay so he can summon the Maker and unmake me?

"Stay here. In Isaura," he says, almost gently. "That face belongs to you."

"But . . . my mother," I begin.

"It's not your responsibility to save your mother," he says.

It is, I think. *Isn't it?*

"It's not," he repeats, as if I've spoken aloud.

I shake my head vigorously. "If you just give me her Seerskin."

"That's not possible," he says.

"Why not?" I plead.

Otak looks at me sharply. "You are Isaurian. You are the child of two Seers. What do your hunches tell you?"

But there is nothing in my head. No coalescing of fact and feeling. I am the most ordinary of young men. I don't belong in Isaura. I don't belong on Earth either. I stare at him, drained.

"Her Seerskin is gone," says Otak. "Used up," he adds.

A little squeak of despair escapes me and Otak flinches as if it's physically painful to be in the presence of somebody who feels so much.

"You should have come to me when you first arrived. I could have saved you from all of this," Otak says. His face hardens. "Go back to your world, then.

Adalia and Phaidra are waiting for you at the portal," he says, dismissing me.

Waiting for me at the portal? This entire time? "You *knew* I wouldn't stay."

"Yes," he says.

"Then why did you ask me to?" I shout in frustration.

He hesitates for a moment. "Because you were never asked before."

And there it is again, something against which I am defenseless—the truth. I wasn't asked before. I wasn't consulted. The choice was made for me by my mother and that's how I became Pucker.

"But she'll die if I go back without her skin," I cry.

He considers this for a moment and I swear I see something like sadness flit across his face.

"She was dying here too," he says quietly.

FIFTY-NINE

Cook jumps to her feet when I step into the clearing. Misery distorts her features. "I'm coming with you," she says.

"I know," I say.

"I should have come years ago. I never should have let you and Serena go alone. You were too sick, both of you."

"Yes, all right," I say. I just want her to stop talking. I can't pay attention to her right now. I'm too focused on Phaidra. She's sitting on a little boulder, her face turned to the side. Does she hate me?

"Phaidra," I breathe.

Phaidra stands. I walk toward her. Pine needles crunch beneath my feet.

"Stop," she says loudly, holding up her hand.

Desperation balloons inside me, filling me with white heat. There will be no taking back what I've done. No second chances. Then suddenly, miraculously, Phaidra's face begins to soften.

"Stop hating yourself," she says.

"I can't," I say. I shut my eyes. I want to be in the dark where she is. I would give up the light for her.

"You have to," she says. "It's enough now. Enough," she says, stepping forward.

When I see her coming toward me, relief, ridiculous and uncomplicated, begins to wash over me. A gentle tide, it laps at my feet.

Then she's in my arms and there is one kiss, there is one girl—there is one love.

· PART ·
FOUR

SIXTY

IT'S NEARLY MIDNIGHT WHEN WE get back to Peacedale. Cook, Phaidra, and I walk down the deserted streets in stunned silence. Dressed in our Isaurian garb, we look like refugees from *The Scarlet Letter*. I can hear Cook breathing heavily as she tries to take it all in: the streetlights buzzing, the July smell of fresh tar and creosote, the roar of I-95.

I haven't touched my face, but I know the scars have returned. I felt it happen as we traveled through the portal. There was something strangely soothing about it. It didn't hurt; it felt tender, like somebody draping cool, wet gauze on my cheeks. I think of Patrick's mother, Clara—the way she would warn me before she peeled off my skin with tweezers.

Our house is just outside of town. About twenty minutes later I'm standing on my porch. I peer through the mesh of the screen door and slowly turn the knob. The floorboards creak, announcing my arrival.

"Thomas?" My mother's voice floats down the stairs. "Is that you?"

"Yes," I say, but I don't move. *Now* I feel my face— the weight of the scars. They burrow themselves into my flesh. A sob escapes from my throat.

"Oh, my boy," my mother cries softly. And then I'm running up the stairs, I'm standing in the doorway of her room—I'm kneeling at her side.

SIXTY-ONE

I AWAKE TO THE SMELL of waffles and bolt upright. I have a hunch something is terribly wrong. My intuition is coiled up inside me like a spring.

I jump out of bed and run into the kitchen. Phaidra, Cook, and Huguette are sitting around the table, talking. They dip back in unison when they see me standing there. I am not looking my best. My hair is flattened from sleep; my jeans ride low on my hips. I'm concave, a pile of bones. I've barely been able to eat since we returned.

"What's happened?" I ask hurriedly.

"Nothing. She had a rough night, but she's okay," says Huguette.

Cook gets up and pours me a cup of coffee. "Sit," she says.

I go over and kiss Phaidra on the cheek and she presses my hand to her face for a moment before letting it go.

It's been nearly eight days since I returned home, and

my mother is still alive. She should be dead by now, but somehow she's managed to hold on. She tells us it's because we're all here. That we've made a wall of love that keeps the visions out. But all of us know that's a lie. The visions are sneaky and relentless. They will smother her one night when we step out of the room.

Here's how the days have passed:

Cook makes breakfast. I bring in a tray to my mother. I sit down on the edge of her bed and we have long, winding, circuitous conversations that last hours, sometimes until dark. We've had a lot of work to do, peeling back the layers of truth. But we have: we've shed the layers one by one until all that remains is a shining nugget of devotion. Her devotion to me. Mine to her. This is undisputed. This is all that matters. Everything else we have done, all the mistakes we have made, all the lies we have told, all the ways we have hurt each other have ceased to matter.

The doorbell rings. Huguette raises her eyebrows silently at me. I shake my head. I don't want to answer it. It rings again, reverberating insistently through the kitchen. I frown and take a sip of coffee, waiting for the footsteps to go away.

"Answer the frigging door, Quicksilver," a voice yells. A hand rattles the knob impatiently.

I freeze. It's Patrick.

"I know you're in there," he says. "There have been sightings."

"Damn," I whisper under my breath. I went out last night for groceries. Somebody must have seen me.

"I'm coming in," he yells. "I'm using my key."

"Don't," I say, but it's too late, I hear his footsteps racing up the stairs, and then he's in the kitchen, bewilderment and hurt spreading across his face when he sees all of sitting around the table.

"Guess my invitation got lost in the mail," he says.

He looks at Cook. She's still wearing her Isaurian clothes: the long clay-colored skirt, the high-necked blouse.

He turns to me. "How was Disneyland, asshole?"

"I wasn't in Disneyland," I say softly.

"No kidding," he says, his eyes falling on Phaidra.

"I couldn't tell you where I was going," I say.

"Why not?" he fires back at me.

"You wouldn't have believed it," I say.

Patrick shakes his head. "You underestimate me," he says. "You always have." Then he clatters down the stairs again. A minute later we hear two sets of feet coming back. My hunch is uncoiling now, stretching to its full length.

"Found her wandering around outside," Patrick says. A young woman follows him into the kitchen.

She's dressed identically to Cook. My mouth drops open in shock—it's Alice, the Maker. Patrick gives her a gentle push forward.

"You feel things," Alice says to me.

"Uh, yes," I stammer.

"Like love?"

"Yes," I tell her. Why is she questioning me? Has she come to hurt us? To make us go back?

"Regret?" she asks.

I blink. I feel like I've stepped forward although I haven't moved, not one inch.

"I feel regret too," Alice says to me.

Phaidra unfolds herself gracefully and stands.

"Why have you come, Alice?" She asks the question I can't seem to get out of my mouth.

"Because I have Serena's skin," Alice says.

Phaidra gasps. "Where?"

Alice frowns. "You can't see it?"

"I'm blind, remember?" says Phaidra.

"I'm not talking about that kind of sight," says Alice. She walks up to Phaidra and takes her hand. Gently she places it on her heart. Phaidra shudders, trying to pull her hand away, but Alice is insistent and then suddenly Phaidra's face transforms. It glows luminously clear.

"My God, Thomas," Phaidra whispers. "She *does* have it."

Alice turns to me. "I'm wearing it."

SIXTY-TWO

ON ALICE'S THIRTEENTH BIRTHDAY SHE was informed by the Ministry that not only would she be the next Maker, but she had been the lead candidate since the day of her birth. *Candidate:* a word that made her sick to her stomach, especially since she didn't know that she had been in the running for anything.

"Smile," Otak said. Didn't she know that she'd won?

"Won *what*?" she asked belligerently.

Otak considered her through the wreath of his pipe smoke. He was wondering if perhaps he had made a mistake. He had already foreseen that she would grow up to be a powerful Seer in her own right. She had that, and she had the right parents, and she had a kind of shine, an undeniable charisma.

What he didn't know (what he couldn't know, because not even he was powerful enough to see into her cells) was that she was hard-wired for empathy—empathy that would one day put forth tentative little shoots, sprout ten-drils, and grow like a weed, spreading through her, until the day she encountered me, looked into my past, and understood how we were connected. She knew who I was the moment she touched me. All of my efforts to keep my memories from her had failed.

Something ended the day that she Changed me: her ability to keep things outside herself anymore.

And just what did happen on her thirteenth birthday? What did Otak say to her parents? How did he break the news? For it was not widely known, in fact, it was a secret that Makers were made, that they were not some mutation, some natural evolution, but instead a result of something much darker. One Seer made twice as powerful by the sac-rifice of another.

"Put this on. It was meant for you," Otak told Alice.

He held out my mother's Seerskin, draped over his arms like it was a great treasure: the royal robes of a monarch, the priestly garments of a pope. He did not tell her whose skin it was. He simply told her that this was how it had been done, for years, since the Great War. This was now her duty, her honor. From this day forward she would wear two skins, her own, which allowed her to see into the future, and a second one on top of that—my mother's.

"But why?" Alice asked him.

Otak told her that during the Great War, when the first Seers were flayed of their skins, the Ministry hunted those skins down along with everybody else. They managed to recover a few that hadn't already been shredded. They had every intention of returning them to their owners.

"What happened next was an accident," Otak explained to Alice.

What the Ministry found out was that when one of their Seers handled those fragile flayed skins, when she so much as touched one, her powers grew much stronger. She could not only see into the future but into the past—and change it.

And so the first Maker came into existence.

The Ministry managed to recover five skins during the war. These skins were hidden away, and when the first Maker died, another one of the skins was brought out and a new Maker was made. This happened three more times, until Alice's predecessor used up the last of the Great War skins. When she died, there was only my mother's skin left, and it was given to Alice.

Alice stares at us, miserable. "Am I too late?" she asks.

I hear my mother coughing in the next room. "No," I tell her.

"All right, I'll need a knife," she says.

Nobody moves as we all realize what she means: she's going to have to cut the skin off.

"Hurry!" Alice says.

Huguette hustles to the counter. "Is this big enough?" she asks, brandishing a chef's knife.

Alice says fearfully, "A little smaller, I think."

Huguette gives her a paring knife.

Alice grips it in her hand and then looks at me and Phaidra. Her face clouds with worry. "Before I take it off, I want to try and Change you and Phaidra again."

Patrick puts his hand on my back protectively. "*Change* them?" he says.

"Heal Thomas's face," Alice says impatiently. "Give Phaidra back her sight."

I stare at her. I try to make a sound, but nothing comes out. I can't allow myself to hope. But foolishly I do.

"But my mother," I protest.

"Don't you want to be healed?" Alice snaps. "I'm still a Maker. I can change you back before I take off Serena's skin, but we've got to hurry. Her skin is losing its power. *I'm* losing my power!"

Phaidra pushes me forward. "You first, Thomas," she says.

"No, you go," I say.

"Decide!" shouts Alice.

"Phaidra," I say, thrusting her in front of me.

Alice nods and places her hands on Phaidra's chest. Phaidra begins to quake and whips her head back violently. Once, twice, three times as the Maker reels back the years. Five long minutes pass. Then slowly Phaidra blinks and comes to.

She searches for me first. Her eyes grow wide and then she quickly collects herself, but not before I've registered her shock at my burns. I remember the first time I saw Phaidra. My panic. She was so beautiful I couldn't let her see me before I was Changed. I feel that same way now. I turn from her in shame.

"Quick," Phaidra cries. "Do Thomas."

But Alice is shaking her head and looking down at the ground. Alice is crying.

"No!" shouts Phaidra.

"Remorse," says Alice, making a fist. "Heartbreak," she whispers, her eyes studded with tears. "I'm sorry. Thomas, it's too late."

I stare at her dismally. "I knew it," I say softly. Here, then, is my fate. I cannot outrun it. I cannot outwit it.

Alice thrusts the knife at Phaidra. "Quick, cut it off," she says.

Phaidra takes the knife and Alice walks forward,

unbuttoning her shirt. I squeeze my eyes shut, but still I hear the horrible sound of the knife cutting into skin. It sounds exactly like fire. A gathering. A puckering.

When I open my eyes, I see Alice stepping out of my mother's skin like she is taking off a pair of stockings. She rolls the skin down her ankles.

"Here," she says, holding it out to me.

It's a weird, gelatinous thing, as soft as cashmere, as translucent as a jellyfish, powdery like a latex glove.

"Quick," she says.

I run into my mother's room, everyone following at my heels. My mother looks up at me, delirious. She doesn't know if she's dreaming or this is real. She reaches up and tenderly touches my face.

"Thomas," she says. Then her eyes grow wide as if she doesn't recognize me. She stares at me in amazement. "Shining Thomas," she whispers.

Then she passes out.

Hurriedly I drape the skin over her body and press it down into her flesh, trying to make it stick.

"Nothing's happening," I cry out.

"Give it a moment to remember her," says Cook, and then finally the skin sinks down into her, enveloping her body like a caul.

The transformation is immediate and profound, and

we all stare at her in awe. She is beautiful. She is protected. A hundred tiny stars sewn into her flesh. In front of our eyes they sink in, fade, until there's nothing there but the faintest memory of their glimmer.

My mother turns onto her side and sighs. She drifts off into sleep, peaceful and without visions for the first time in eleven years. She has finally got what she wanted. Everyone has gotten what they wanted.

Except me.

SIXTY-THREE

ALMOST SIX WEEKS LATER I wander into the kitchen and pour myself the last dregs of the coffee. It's late August. In a few days I start my senior year of high school.

I have the house to myself. My mother and Cook have walked into town.

Phaidra moved out last week; both she and Alice are staying with Huguette. I wanted Phaidra to live with us, but our apartment is too small. She's going to attend my high school in the fall, and, apart from the seven hours or so we sleep each night, we are inseparable.

"Thomas!" I hear Cook yell from outside.

I look out the window. She holds up a pink cardboard box from the doughnut shop. "Breakfast," she sings.

They clomp up the stairs and when my mother enters the kitchen and sees me, she gasps.

I pat my head, trying to smooth my hair down. "That bad?"

"It's not your hair," whispers Cook. She, too, is staring.

My mother nods, her eyes moist. "It was my last vision. I didn't dream it, Adalia," she says.

"Dream what?" I ask, slightly annoyed. It's entirely too early in the morning to be getting so emotional.

"Go look in the mirror," she says.

"I don't want to go look in the mirror," I say, but my heart is beginning to thud against my ribs.

"Humor me," she says.

In the time it takes me to walk from the kitchen to the bathroom, I have a hunch. My hunch is that I will be having many more hunches. Hunches that are right most of the time, because this is what happens to Isaurian Seers who live on Earth. They can't see into the future anymore, but they still have their intuition.

What I see when I look in the mirror is that while I've

slept, I've started to grow a Seerskin. A skin that, while it doesn't completely hide my scars, softens them somehow, makes me look almost normal.

My mother walks into the bathroom and strokes my cheek softly.

"You have the kind of beauty that only comes from having suffered," she says.

My eyes fill with tears and I wipe them away savagely with the back of my hand so I can gaze at my image and see that it's true, that it's *not* a dream.

I have gotten my face, finally. It's not perfect. It's not without flaw. But it's the face that I've earned.

Suddenly the phone rings, startling us all. "I'll get it," says my mother. She walks briskly away. I hear her pick it up, listen for a while, and say nothing in response. Slowly she puts the receiver back in its cradle.

She walks back into the bathroom. "That was a crank call," she says softly.

I close my eyes, the old despair weighing down my limbs.

"I'm sorry, Thomas. I didn't know what to tell them," she says.

"What did they want?" asks Cook.

My mother pauses. "They wanted to know if our refrigerator was running."

It's Cook who cracks a smile first. Then my mother. And then we begin to laugh, and once we start, we cannot stop.

It's as if we're laughing ourselves alive.

ACKNOWLEDGMENTS

Abiding thanks to my editor, Eloise Flood, and all the folks at Razorbill. I am deeply grateful to my agent, Charlotte Sheedy, and to my writing group: Caroline Paul and Eric Martin. Also, a heartfelt thanks to everyone who helped along the way: Elizabeth Leahy; Joanne Hartman; Renee Schoepflin; Debi Echlin; Dominique Niespolo; Cindi Brogan; my parents, Sarah and Vasant Gideon; and my two Bens.

About the Author

MELANIE GIDEON is the author of *The Map That Breathed*, a New York Public Library Book for the Teen Age. She lives in Northern California with her husband and son.